A SERIES OF DEFEATS

BARRY NORMAN was show-business editor of the *Daily Mail* until 1971, when he became redundant. He describes this as 'the best thing that ever happened to me', since it has enabled him to turn his hand to a wide variety of activities. He is, or has been, a TV critic and show-business interviewer for *The Times*, a regular columnist for the *Guardian*, sports writer for the *Observer* and scriptwriter for 'Flook' in the *Daily Mail*. In addition, he has written and presented *The Hollywood Greats* and *Film '78* for BBC TV. His other novels include *To Nick a Good Body*, *End Product* and *Tales of the Redundance Kid*.

Despite all this, he still finds time to play cricket for the Hertfordshire village where he lives with his wife and two daughters.

Barry Norman

A SERIES OF DEFEATS

Arrow Books

Arrow Books Ltd
3 Fitzroy Square, London W1P 6JD

An imprint of the Hutchinson Publishing Group

London Melbourne Sydney Auckland
Wellington Johannesburg and agencies
throughout the world

First published by Quartet Books 1977
Arrow edition 1979

Made and printed in Great Britain by
William Collins Sons & Co Ltd Glasgow

ISBN 0 09 919640 9

'A man who gives a good account of himself is probably lying, since any life when viewed from the inside is simply a series of defeats'

– George Orwell

For Diana – at long last

1. SUICIDE!

The razor's edge lay sharp and cool across his throat, just above the Adam's apple. It wouldn't be difficult – a little pressure, a swift flick of the right wrist and 'Aargh!', thud, crash, a body on the floor and blood all over the bathroom.

Goodbye, Henry Tyson.

Henry Tyson looked at himself in the mirror and his face stared back, gloomy and pensive. Was he holding the razor in the right place, that was the question. Should it be above the Adam's apple or below it, or even on it? He took his right hand away and pressed his Adam's apple with his left. A strange croaking sound came from his throat. It was difficult to breathe when you pressed like that.

He looked at his reflection again. Not a bad face, really; a little puffier, a little plumper than it had been a few years back. Ah, but naturally. He had been young then . . . Still, his hair was all right, neither thinning nor receding and just the same indeterminate brownish colour it had always been. It could do with cutting of course, but . . . well, that would be someone else's problem soon.

Perhaps they'd give it a trim before they laid him out in the mortuary. And they'd probably put a bit of lipstick and rouge on him to make him look more lifelike. He didn't fancy that very much. Then they'd dress him in his best suit – the navy-blue three-piece with the pinstripe – twist his mouth into a happy grin, cross his hands over his chest, hoist his collar up to hide the gash in his throat and call the mourners in for a good old cry-up.

There were tears in the eyes that stared back at him from the mirror and the deep breath he took shivered with grief.

On that day, when they laid him out, the chief mourner wouldn't be weeping along with the rest. He'd be lying there, in the coffin, covered in rouge and lipstick, grinning up at the ceiling. But the others . . . would they really grieve, would they really miss him? Timmy would, of course. It would be sad for Timmy, terribly sad.

The tears left Henry's eyes and made their way slowly down his cheeks. He brushed them away with his hand.

Sue, though, would she miss him? He hoped so. By God, he did. He hoped she'd be well and truly sorry . . .

He took another of those shuddering breaths and looked at himself for the last time in the mirror.

Henry Tyson. Aged thirty-five. Or, to be exact, aged thirty-five years, two months, three weeks and four days. Mr Nothing from Nowhere. A failure. Goodbye, Henry Tyson.

He raised his right hand and slowly laid the razor across his throat . . .

'Oh, God, not again.' He hadn't noticed Sue come in and the sound of her voice startled him. The razor jerked and a single drop of blood fell into the washbasin.

'Now look what you've done!' He was furious. 'You've made me cut myself.'

'I thought that was the whole idea.' She was leaning against the door frame, crisp and attractive in a dark blue shirt and a short white skirt. She was a rather tall, rather pretty girl with pale blonde hair and very calm grey eyes. Behind the calmness there was a glint of something else, humour perhaps, though Henry sometimes had an uncomfortable suspicion that it was more likely mockery, directed at him.

'I suppose this is another practice run,' she said. 'That's three in the last month to my certain knowledge. When are you actually going to do the job? Try and make it a day when the char comes in, will you? Blood's so messy to clear up.'

'Very funny.'

'Well, get on with it. I'm fed up with this morbid messing about. Do you want me to give you a hand?'

'Listen,' Henry said, 'when I decide to do it, I'll do it my way, without any help from you.'

'Please yourself.'

Another drop of blood fell into the bowl.

'Look at this! Blood all over the place.'

'Here.' She ripped a tiny corner from the toilet roll and handed it to him.

'Oh, charming. A lovely sight I'll be, walking round London with lavatory paper strung round my neck like a bloody scarf.'

She shrugged. 'There's some cotton wool in the cabinet.'

Better still there was a tin of adhesive dressings, and he selected a very large square piece and carefully removed the protective strip of gauze.

Sue watched him, quizzically. 'I suppose you realize,' she said, 'that you wouldn't need that much plaster if you'd been shot.'

'I know what I need.' Henry stretched his neck and put the plaster gingerly in place, gazing down his nose at his reflection. 'I bleed a lot when I'm cut. I've got sensitive skin.'

He had put his razor on the window-sill and Sue went over to examine it. 'Good God,' she said. 'Fancy trying to cut your throat with a *safety* razor. You could hack away all day without getting past the skin.'

Henry said nothing. He held out his hand, she put the razor in it and he carried on shaving. Sue went back to the door and leaned against it. It did not displease her at all to note that the muscles in his neck were hard with tension.

'I'll tell you what,' she said. 'I'll buy you a cut-throat razor for Christmas. Then you'll be able to do a thorough job.'

'Oh, shut up.'

'But of course if you don't want to wait that long . . . Hey, I've got an idea. Why don't you fill the bath with lovely warm water, get into it and cut your wrists? They say it's quite painless, almost pleasant, really and . . .'

'Shut up! Shut up! Shut up! Leave me alone! For God's sake leave me alone!' His voice soared to a dramatic crescendo on the final syllable and at the same time he hurled his razor violently to the floor. It bounced back and hit him on the foot but he hardly noticed the pain. 'You're so bloody smart, aren't you? So bloody funny? You don't understand, do you? You don't know what's going on in here.' He jabbed an index finger against his forehead. 'The frustration . . . the . . . oh, for God's sake get out.'

She watched him coolly, smiling, with that humorous – or perhaps mocking – glint in her eyes. 'You'd better get a move on,' she said, 'or you'll be late for work.'

The door closed behind her. He glared at it, trembling, for a moment before stooping to retrieve his razor. There was a half-inch gash on his right instep and blood was trickling down between his toes. He put more plaster on the wound and stood and surveyed himself in the mirror. His eyes stared wildly back at him. Hurt eyes, they seemed to him. Stricken, even. There's suffering in that face, he thought, but she doesn't see it and if she saw it she wouldn't care.

He sighed heavily and washed the soap from his cheeks.

It was hard to say what had caused it. Nothing. Or a lot of things. Little things, probably. Anyway, they had been bickering now for quite a while – since his birthday, really. Or the day that agent had sent Henry's novel back with a snotty letter. Bloody cheek.

Was that before his birthday or after? After, not that it mattered really. Both misfortunes had occurred at more or less the same time and they had hit him equally hard. Thirty-five – and rejected. Happy birthday, Henry.

And then the bickering had started. Not total war. Not a punch-up. Just the usual marital skirmishing, verbal scratching, words thrown back and forth, sharp as thorns, piercing the skin, though not the flesh. No fatal wounds inflicted; certainly no single fatal wounds.

There had been many such skirmishes in their eight years of marriage but this one was different. It had lasted longer for a start. Usually these things were over, the peace treaty sealed by a joyous romp in bed, within a few days. This time though there had been no treaty because nobody had sued for peace and so it had dragged on with minor escalations here and there and just lately there had been an entirely new development. The irritable exchanges had died away, to be replaced by a sullen silence. It was like two armies digging in for the winter, securing their positions and watching each other across no man's land. For the past week a state of cold politeness had prevailed.

But then this morning, as if the winter were over and the spring campaign about to open, Sue had started it all again by asking him to do the school run. The bloody school run!

'Do what? You know what you can do with the school run, don't you?'

'Yeah? What can I do with the school run?' The glint in her eyes was unmistakably anger. Pale blonde hair fell in silky sweeps around her face.

'You know.'

'No, I don't know. You tell me.'

'You can stick the . . .'

'*Pas devant l'enfant!*'

Timmy had come into their bedroom, four years old, all tousled hair and huge eyes, Pinky and Perky all over his pyjamas and a Teddy Bear in his arms.

'*Merde!*'

'Oh, delightful. What a gentleman your daddy is, to be sure, Timmy.'

'Well, I'm not doing the bloody school run and that's that.'

And then he had gone to the bathroom to cut his throat.

2. BREAKFAST AT HENRY'S

'Do you think I'm going mad?' Henry asked, when he got downstairs.

'If you like.'

'What do you mean – if I like?'

'If it pleases you to think I think you're going mad, then all right, I think you're going mad.'

'You're not much help, you know,' he said sadly.

Sue went into the kitchen and started banging saucepans about. Henry sat down in the dinette. Dinette – what a daft word. It wasn't much more than a cupboard, really, though Sue had decorated it nicely – bright wallpaper and cheerful carpet.

'Walter Wall,' Henry said, thinking about the carpet and trying to make conversation. 'He'd be a carpet salesman, wouldn't he? Like Lars Torders, the Norwegian barman . . .'

No answer. He picked up a spoon and held it near his mouth, like a microphone. 'Do *you* wake up in the mornings bad-tempered and out-of-sorts?' he declaimed in a TV–commercial voice. 'Are you irritable? Are you liverish? Do *you* ignore your poor long-suffering sod of a husband when he asks you a civil question? Do you? Then get stuffed!'

Still no response. Henry sat down at the breakfast table and took a quick look through the morning paper. They hadn't used his story about the model whose boobs had fallen out of her dress in the Dorchester. He wasn't too disappointed. It was a lousy story, reeking of publicity stunt. They'd been lousy boobs, too, come to that, small and scrawny. They couldn't really have fallen out of her dress; they must have been pushed.

'I've been thinking,' he said, addressing the clatter in the kitchen. 'You know what's the matter with us? We don't communicate any more. We talk but we don't communicate. There's a cotton wool curtain between us.' He rather liked that last touch.

Sue said: 'Oh, Lor'. Look who's been reading the *Observer* again.'

Henry shook his head sorrowfully but otherwise ignored the jibe. 'Well, it's true. You don't know what goes on inside me, do you? You don't know what I feel or think.'

Cutlery rattled in the kitchen.

'We'll have to do something, you know,' he said. 'We can't go on like this. When did we last have it off? Can *you* remember? I can't. It's not good enough. Our marriage will be on the rocks soon and I put it all down to lack of communication. It's a great problem, communication, one of the great problems of our age.'

He stared thoughtfully out of the window at the little back garden. The lawn needed a cut; it was knee-high and choked with dandelions – but where did he get the time to go shoving lawn-mowers about?

'Time's the problem,' he said. 'We never get time to talk. I mean really talk. All we do is exchange noises – hello, what's on telly?, pass the salt, how's your father? Sounds, that's all we make. We never *say* anything any more. We're drifting apart, you and I.'

'Do you want two eggs or one?'

'What?'

'Two eggs or one?'

'God Almighty!' This was too much. 'You haven't listened to a word I've been saying, have you? Damn you! Don't talk to me about eggs. Here am I trying to save our marriage and all you can talk about is bloody eggs.' He put his head in his hands and stared desolately at the table-cloth. Red and white gingham, it was. 'Are they boiled or fried?'

'Boiled.'

'I'll have two, then.'

Sue brought in the eggs and Timmy, and the three of them ate in silence, or as much silence as was possible when their son was eating. Then she said; 'Go and put your coat on, darling. Nearly time for school.'

Timmy went out, wiping his yolk-encrusted mouth on his sleeve.

'You know the real trouble?' Sue said to Henry. 'Between you and me, I mean? It's you. You're the one who's breaking up our marriage if anyone is.'

'Nonsense.'

'It isn't. You've been very odd lately, ever since your birthday. Full of self-pity.'

'I don't wish to discuss that,' Henry said, loftily.

'Well, it's true. You seem to think just because you're thirty-five and not world-famous that you're a failure. It's absolutely absurd.'

'Oh, sure. It's all right for you to talk. How old are you – twenty-nine? You're not even thirty yet, for Chrissake. You're still young *and* you're a success. But I'm thirty-five, thirty-five's old these days, and what have I ever achieved? Nothing. Even that book I wrote was no good.'

'Nobody said that.'

'That crappy agent did. He said it was unsaleable.'

'In its present form. That's what he said and it doesn't mean –'

'It's all right for you,' Henry said again. 'You don't know what failure is. You don't know the frustration. Who was it said that if a man hadn't made his mark by thirty he never would? Beaverbrook, wasn't it? Some old git like that, anyway. And he was right. And what's more he was talking about bloody thirty, not thirty-fi –'

'Oh, for heaven's sake!' Her voice was sharp with exasperation. 'Writing yourself off at thirty-five. It's ridiculous. And why thirty-five, for God's sake? Everybody else gets neurotic about being thirty or forty. But not you. Oh, no, you have to be different. You have to pick on thirty-five. What's so bloody awful about thirty-five?'

'Everything,' Henry said, hurling his arms about. 'Can't you see that? Isn't it obvious? Thirty-five is middle age, exact, precise, true middle age. It's the most crucial point in a man's life, a . . . a watershed. The day a man becomes thirty-five he's left his youth behind for ever, every tiny little sodding scrap of it. I'm a middle-aged man, halfway to my three score years and ten and getting closer every minute. From here on it's a straight run – downhill to the grave.'

Sue shook her head sadly. 'You're out of your mind, of course,' she said. 'You ought to run, not walk, to your nearest psychiatrist, that's what you ought to do. Look, let's get this into perspective.

You want to be a writer, okay? Okay, well, let's look at some writers. Look at Galsworthy. He hadn't written anything when he was thirty-five . . .'

'Sod Galsworthy,' Henry said. 'You know I can't read Galsworthy. Smug capitalist swine.'

'All right.' There was a hard, brittle note of patience in her voice. 'Forget Galsworthy. Take Shaw instead. Now Shaw was over forty before he wrote his first play.'

'Right,' Henry said, triumphantly. 'Right. Plays – you're talking about plays. I don't want to write plays. Plays are different. I want to write books, novels . . .'

She nodded, slowly. 'All right.' She felt sure of herself now because she had just remembered the one argument to which he could have no answer. 'What about Chandler then? You can't sod Chandler because you're potty about him and don't you dare even try to deny it. And yet Chandler didn't write a book until he was fifty. You've got years to go yet.'

Henry was silent for a moment. He'd forgotten about Chandler. 'Very well,' he said. 'Very well. I'll grant you Chandler. But don't you see? Can't you grasp it even now? He's the exception that proves the rule, that's what he is. The exception that proves the glorious, bitter, immutable rule. There's only one Chandler, whereas the world is full of people like me.'

'Oh, I hope not,' Sue said. 'Please God, I do hope not.' She looked at him steadily and rather sadly. 'Well, I give up,' she said. 'I just give up.'

And at this moment of capitulation, while Henry was wondering why the victory he had just gained was so very unsatisfactory, Timmy came back wearing a scarlet anorak and carrying his Teddy Bear. 'Ready, Mummy,' he said.

'Good boy,' Sue said, welcoming this timely interruption. She fetched a flannel from the kitchen and wiped the débris of breakfast from her son's face. Over her shoulder she said: 'Are you going to do the school run for me or aren't you? You've got plenty of time.'

Henry spread some marmalade on the last piece of toast. 'We've been through that and the answer is still no.'

'I don't see why. It would be a great help to me and it's not much to ask you to do for your son.'

Gutturally, through the toast, Henry said: 'I don't mind taking Timmy to school. I don't even mind taking the other kids.' He swallowed. 'It's the mothers I can't stand. They make me feel such a fool. I don't know what's happened to women these days. They're so . . . aggressive. Cocky. It's an emasculating experience, that school run.'

'How would you know?' she snapped. 'You've never done it.'

'Yes, I have. Once. All those women looked at me like I was henpecked.'

'Oh, you're impossible.'

She swept out the way women do when they're cross and he could hear her bustling about in the hallway. In a few minutes she reappeared, dressed for going out.

'You won't be late tonight, will you? There's that party, remember.'

'Which one's that – the publishing one for your book?' Henry poured himself some more coffee.

'No, that's tomorrow. You know it is. God, you're irritating. Sometimes I think you do it on purpose, just to annoy me.'

He chuckled happily. 'Which party's this then?'

'The one the girls are giving for me. At Lorna Collins's house.'

'Ah, yes. Honouring the celebrated author in their midst. What jolly fun. All right, I'll be early.'

'You'd better be.' She went away dragging Timmy behind her.

'Take that Teddy Bear away from him,' Henry yelled after them. 'I don't want him growing up into a poof. And don't give me any crap about Gay Lib either. It may be legal these days but it's not necessarily what every man wants for his son. Good God, Timmy's pushing five – he ought to be playing with guns at his age!'

The door slammed and in a moment the car started up. Henry sat where he was for a while, smoking a cigarette and thinking. Then he shook his head and went into the kitchen to do the washing-up.

3. SCENES FROM DOMESTIC LIFE . . . I

'I remember. I remember . . .'

Four days after his thirty-fifth birthday, the agent sent his book back and the bank sent him a statement. It was like being coshed on the back of the head at the precise moment that someone else was kicking him in the stomach.

He went to work that morning in a mood of severe depression and returned feeling a good deal worse, having spent the day interviewing a twenty-one-year-old tycoon of the pop music industry, who owned a flat in Park Lane, a Rolls-Royce and, as far as Henry could tell, an inexhaustible supply of delicious little dollies. He appeared to have one for home consumption, another to lighten his working hours and a third permanently established in his car, so that wherever he went he would never be caught without one. He also remarked, quite casually, that he liked to trade them in for newer models every couple of months or so.

Henry was impressed. He looked and listened with cynical disbelief but he was impressed all the same.

When he got home there was only bread and cheese for supper because Sue had been too busy to shop that day; Timmy had hurled a brick through the garage window and the same agent who had declined Henry's book with perfunctory thanks had phoned to say he had sold the paperback rights of Sue's.

Henry had eaten his bread and cheese in a markedly morose fashion, sighing from time to time to underline the fact, for there was no point in being morose if nobody noticed.

After a while Sue had said: 'All right, what is it?'

I'm fed up, that's all.'

Still worried about being thirty-five?'

'Do you have to keep reminding me?' It was odd, though, how hard it had hit him. Thirty he had taken more or less in his stride. At thirty he had still felt himself to be on the way up; a late developer, possibly, but nevertheless an eager young man with places to go. Even at thirty-four years, eleven months, three weeks and six days he had felt youthful, not exactly a boy perhaps but comparatively young even so. On the right side of middle age anyway. The following day, however, he was thirty-five and that was suddenly old. It seemed to him that he was even beginning to look old and certainly he felt old. There was a sense of panic, of time passing by and promise unfulfilled. What had he done with those vital, glorious, crucial years of youth? Where was the mark he had left on the world? If he had died that very morning, his birthday, what would anyone have found to say of him except, Henry who?' At a time when all doors opened to the young he had somehow contrived to reach the immense age of thirty-five with nothing to show for it except an overdraft. That morning he had decided not to wear his favourite denim suit for fear that people would point him out to each other as an ageing trendy trying to defy the passage of time.

'I don't know, I don't know.' He had got up and prowled about while Sue sat at her drawing board making sketches for her second book and listened with a kind of affectionate resignation. 'I think I was born too early or too late or both,' he said. 'God, if only I were *younger*.'

She began to ink in a pencilled outline, her tongue sticking out childishly from the corner of her mouth. 'What would you do if you were?'

'Oh, I'd . . . I'd go running around, sleeping with anybody, being irresponsible. You don't know how I *long* to be irresponsible – but I'm too old for it and I've been brought up the wrong way. I've been taught all my life that a man gets a job and sticks to it and marries a wife and sticks to her and raises a family and sticks to that.'

'Quite right,' she said approvingly.

'Is it?' He took an apple in his hand and tried to crush it, but his fingers weren't strong enough and after bruising it a bit he put it back in the bowl. 'I'm not so sure. I think all these promiscuous kids who carry the Pill like I carry Polo mints are happier than I am. If only I'd been born a few years later, just five or six – or earlier, I wouldn't have minded that either. If I was leading my respectable, inhibited, worry-packed, middle-class life at a time when everyone else was doing the same I'd have been all right. I wouldn't have challenged it or doubted its values. But it's being respectable and stifled in an age when people only a bit younger than I am are having the wildest, most glorious ball in history that I can't stand. I feel old and I want to feel young.'

There was a brief, cool silence. 'I see,' she said, frostily. 'I'm stifling you, am I?'

'No,' he cried in despair. 'Why do you have to take it personally all the time? It's not just you, it's everything.'

'Then do something about it,' she said.

'What? Tell me that. What?'

'Haven't you any initiative?'

'No. That's the whole point. I've not been trained for initiative. None of my generation was. We're the pre-Beatles generation . . .'

'The Beatles!' Sue murmured. 'You're talking about history.'

'Right! I belong to history. My entire generation belongs to history. We were never teenagers, you know, people of my age. We were adolescents. Teenagers hadn't been invented then. We weren't pampered and pandered to and wooed by the advertisers. We never had any money for a start. We were just people going through the awkward age before plunging into steady, boring, respectable adulthood. Trained for initiative? I should bloody think so. All we were trained for was to be solid and reliable.'

She took a thick, soft pencil and began to fill in the shadows on her picture. 'Didn't do much of a job on you then, did they?'

He stopped prowling and turned his anguished face heavenwards in search of support. 'Don't you *understand*? Have you no sympathy?'

'Well . . . you're just talking nonsense. All these kids you keep envying so much – how are they better off than you?'

'What do you mean? Haven't you seen them? They work when they feel like it and loaf when they don't. They're ruthless and selfish and marvellous. They live for today and bugger tomorrow. They don't tie themselves up with mortgages and insurance policies. They don't worry themselves sick because they've got an overdraft.'

'You're mad,' she said. 'You don't know what you're talking about.'

'Yes, I do! These kids are *living* and I'm not. I've never lived. In no time at all I'll be a little old middle-aged man and I'll never have been anything else. Dammit, I'm middle-aged now. I'm thirty-five and I'm middle-aged and I've been middle-aged ever since I left school.'

'Mad,' Sue murmured, shaking her head sadly. 'Barmy.'

'No, I'm not. I'm the sane one. Don't you see? We've gone wrong, we've all gone wrong. "Get a job, get a house, get a car, get the strength of the insurance companies around you." What's all this got to do with life?'

Sue laid her drawing aside and propped her chin on her hands. 'You really haven't the faintest idea what you're talking about, you know. This glorious, promiscuous life you want so much, this never-ending youthful ball – you missed all that years ago. I think you really do belong to history. They ought to stuff you and stick you in a museum as a perfect specimen of an extinct species. Those wild, happy-go-lucky days you envy so deeply are all gone. The Age of Aquarius is over. This is the Age of Austerity, the Age of Inflation. Those kids aren't going around having a ball, they're going around looking for work. There's unemployment in the land, my son. They're all on the dole.'

'It's no good,' Henry said. 'You just don't understand.'

Sue got up briskly and started putting her drawing things away. 'Oh, I understand, all right,' she said. 'It's no use talking to you in this mood. You're not thinking, you're just reacting. You're feeling sorry for yourself, that's all.' Quite suddenly she burst into tears. 'And anyway it's jolly unfair to say that I'm stifling you and holding you back and ruining your life.'

'I didn't say that!' he cried, horrified.

'Yes, you *did* and you're a rotten pig!' And she went out and shut the door behind her.

Henry slumped down on the chair she had just vacated and stared gloomily at the carpet. How different, he thought, how very different from the home life of our own dear Queen . . .

4. COUGHLIN

An ugly building just off Fleet Street. Above the door in letters that once were white and now were stained like dingy teeth – *The Daily Journal* and below that in smaller letters, *The Sunday Journal*. A commissionaire in bottle-green picked his teeth on the doorstep.

Inside, a vestibule, large and circular, all chrome, pale wood and rounded edges – the 1930s Ghastly style of architecture.

Two lifts facing each other and from within each of them irate sounds of warring liftmen, roaring like lions from the depths of their lairs.

'You done that on purpose, dincher? You switched it so I 'ad to go up, 'stead of you. You'll do that once too often, mate. Lazy sod.'

'Do what?'

'Lazy sod, I said.'

'Talk to *me* like that! Why, I'll . . .'

'You'll what?'

'You 'eard.'

'Come on, then.'

'Don't think I wouldn't, mate. Talk to me like that.'

'Come on, then.'

'All right, then.'

'All right.'

A dramatic pause, then the combatants emerged, grunting their wrath, old and crippled and leaning heavily on sticks, hobbling fast across the foyer to stand nose to nose, eyes full of rage, chests full of combat ribbons from a long-gone war.

Henry ducked between them – 'Gentlemen, please!' – and walked up the stairs to the third floor.

Here, behind the swing doors that led to the editorial department of the *Daily Journal*, the décor was different. Post-war Utility was the dominating influence. Cream walls covered with posters – 'You can *depend on* the *Daily Journal*' – and exhortations – 'Get it *right*!' Black linoleum pock-marked with the acne of burned-out cigarette ends. Along the corridor grim little offices where the mighty of the paper resided behind grim little metal doors and opaque glass partitions.

And in the centre one huge, open room with colonies of desks bearing phones and typewriters – here the reporters sat and there the sub-editors, yonder the sportswriters, and the gossip writers and the feature writers. Beyond the ranks of the reporters' desks a room with walls of glass wherein sat the news editor and his acolytes, and from within as Henry reached his desk a peremptory yell in a voice accustomed to command: 'Henry!'

He went in.

The news editor, a bald and brutal man, put his hand over the mouthpiece of the telephone into which he had been shouting and looked up. 'You've done the show business beat before, haven't you?'

'Once or twice,' Henry said.

'Do it for the rest of the week, will you? Candlish is sick. 'Flu, I think. Bloody fool. I told him not to sleep with damp women.' The news editor laughed, harshly. The acolytes laughed too. So, to his personal shame, did Henry. There was nothing in his terms of employment to say he had to laugh at the news editor's jokes but he always did. The news editor disliked people who didn't laugh at his jokes.

'Off you go, then.'

Henry went back to his desk. There were only half a dozen reporters in at this time in the morning and one of them said: 'Henry, Coughlin wants to see you. His secretary just phoned.'

'Thanks.' Trepidation plucked at Henry's insides, playing on his nerve-ends like a sitar. Coughlin was the executive editor, a new man lately bought at an inflated salary from a rival paper. Henry didn't like him and he didn't like Henry. 'Wonder what he wants to see me for?'

'Perhaps you're for the chop', the other reporter, Bilbow, said indifferently. 'He's been threatening to make changes.'

'What a source of encouragement and hope you are,' Henry said.

He found Coughlin at the end of the corridor unlocking the door to the executives' washroom.

'You wanted to see me?' he said.

'Ah, yes. It's . . . er . . . Henry, isn't it? Come in.'

'In there?'

'Why not? You can watch me pee.'

'Oh. All right.' Henry followed him in, vaguely intrigued. Perhaps executives peed differently from lesser people. Coughlin, however, took up a traditional stance by the stall in the corner and Henry perched himself on the mahogany windowsill and waited.

Coughlin sighed and said, 'Ah, that's better,' and then he said: 'About that vacancy on the features staff. You applied for the job, didn't you?'

'Yes. I sent a memo to the features editor. I've always wanted to be a feature writer and . . .'

'Yes,' Coughlin said, staring down into the cubicle, his hands on his hips. (Look, Ma, no hands!) 'Yes, well he passed it on to me.'

'Oh.' Henry bit his lip, anxiously. He had set a lot of store by getting that feature-writing job.

'He also showed me that piece you did for him yesterday. I'm sorry to say I didn't think much of it.'

'Really?' Henry said defensively. 'Why not?'

'It's not meaningful.' Meaningful was Coughlin's word of the month.

'I don't understand.'

'It doesn't tell me anything about life,' Coughlin said. 'It doesn't . . . Damn!'

'What's the matter?'

'First Law of Motion – no matter how you shake and shake, the last drop always goes down your trouser-leg. Do you have that trouble?'

'No,' Henry said.

'Really? Maybe it's just me. It always happens with me.' Coughlin went to the washbasin and turned on the hot tap. Along the black marble ledge above the washbasins was ranged a selection of combs, soaps, hand-towels and hair-brushes. The ordinary washrooms merely had blocks of Lifebuoy soap and a roller towel.

Coughlin began to wash his hands vigorously. He was a big man with a touch of Northern Ireland in his voice. He wore Young Executive suits from a shop in King's Road, Chelsea, and he looked younger than his forty-five years.

'It doesn't speak to me, that story of yours. It's not compulsive.' Compulsive, actually, was last month's word but it had lasted longer than most and carried over into this month. Stories had to be meaningful now but they would also get by if they were only compulsive. If they happened to be both, Coughlin practically went berserk with joy. 'It doesn't tell me anything about your problems or my problems.'

Henry didn't think he had ever heard so much drivel in his life. 'It's not supposed to tell you anything about your problems or my problems,' he said, sharply. 'It's about a West Indian bus driver who took his bus over the wrong route. How can you be meaningful about a West Indian bus driver?'

Coughlin looked up from his handwashing and surveyed him coldly in the mirror. 'There's nothing more meaningful than a West Indian bus driver,' he said. 'That's the most meaningful thing there is in our society. Except perhaps a Pakistani bus driver.'

Henry put his hands in his trouser pockets and clenched his fists. He could feel anger building up but he didn't like to show it. Coughlin was not a good man to show anger to.

'It's supposed to be a funny story,' he said.

'I know that. But it's soft. Nicely written, I grant you. But soft. It's not . . . it's not *forcing* its way into the paper. It would be a bloody sight better story if it was funny *and* meaningful. Look, get meaningful, that's all I ask.'

'I don't know how,' Henry said. It was becoming very difficult to keep the anger and frustration out of his voice. 'I don't even known what the damn word means.'

Coughlin threw his hand towel into the basin in a sudden rush of temper. 'Then I don't see any point in continuing this any further. You're simply being obtuse. Look, for Christ's sake, I'm telling you what's wrong with your story, not asking for an argument. What I tell you is not a basis for discussion. It's final. I don't want your opinions. I don't care about your opinions. It's my opinion that counts and in my opinion your story is not . . .'

'Meaningful,' Henry said, between clenched teeth.

'Exactly and I don't want to discuss it any more.' On which note he turned abruptly away and swept out of the washroom, slamming the door behind him.

With his going went much of Henry's anger. He had handled that situation very badly, no doubt about it. He should have said 'Yes, Mr Coughlin' and 'No, Mr Coughlin' and 'Sorry about your trouser leg, Mr Coughlin.' After all, if he could laugh at the news editor's jokes why couldn't he crawl a little to this ageing whizz-kid, who, handled properly, could do him so much good?

Furthermore, he had still not had a definite answer about that vacancy on the features staff and with a view to tackling Coughlin again on the subject, he went to the door only to find that it was jammed and he was unable to open it.

He tried pulling, pushing, rattling the handle and poking at the lock with a blade of his penknife. He even tried shouting 'Help' through the keyhole but nothing happened and nobody came and in the end, just so that it wasn't a total loss, he made use of one of the cubicles. After that he sat on the window-sill and waited, edgy with frustration.

He was still there fifteen minutes later when the door was unlocked from the outside and the editor came in, grey-haired, grey-eyed, grey-suited and sternly magisterial. He seemed surprised to see Henry sitting there.

'What are you doing in here?' he asked.

'Mr Coughlin locked me in,' Henry said.

'Mr Coughlin did? What on earth for?'

'I don't know.'

'Curious thing to do.' The editor frowned thoughtfully into one of the cubicles where the marble pedestals were topped with polished wooden seats as only befitted executive dignity. 'What were you doing in here anyway? This is reserved for senior people.'

'I know. Mr Coughlin invited me in.'

'Why?'

Henry shrugged. 'He said I was to watch him pee.'

'*Did* he?' Another frown. The editor didn't like Coughlin any more than Henry did. He had had the man wished upon him, despite his protests, by the chairman's son. 'Well, I shan't be requiring the same service. You may go.'

'Thank you.'

The editor held the door open and Henry went out. He felt a bit better now.

The reporters' room had filled up a little by the time Henry got back to his desk. Phones ringing, typewriters clacking. People sitting on desks, chatting to each other. Isolated snatches of conversation . . . 'Do you remember the time he threw his socks in the fire in the saloon bar?'

Henry put a cup on his desk and the copy boy filled it with tea from an ancient enamel jug. It was a very large jug, very chipped and the inside was stained a deep and loathsome brown. The letters D.J. were painted on the outside in bright green. There was a theory within the office that the letters stood for *Daily Journal*, since the jug was the property thereof, but Henry knew better. He knew they stood, with beautiful simplicity, for Dirty Jug.

'Ugh,' he said. The tea was lukewarm and stiff with sugar.

At the next desk Bilbow looked up from *The Times*, bluff and North Country and professionally lovable. Everyone loved Bilbow except those who knew him well. 'What are you on?' he asked.

'Show biz. Candlish is ill.'

'Lucky devil. Beats working, that does. If I had my time again I'd be a show business reporter. Steady old round of cocktail parties, free dinners and long-legged starlets wanting their names in the paper at any price. Marvellous.'

'Do me a favour.' The show business beat wasn't like that at all. It was warm gin, other people's egos and publicity men forever on your back. 'What are you on?'

'Old Bailey – the big fraud case. Means drinking with a lot of coppers again. Brown ale and large Scotches.'

'Tough,' Henry said unsympathetically. He couldn't be bothered much with other people's problems at the moment.

'Yeah. Heard who got that features job?'

Henry sat up. 'No. Who?'

'Jennifer Clovis.' Bilbow watched his reaction with malicious pleasure.

'What! She's only been here three months – barely out of school. It's not . . . I asked for that job.'

'I know,' Bilbow said happily.

'Why did she get it? Why not me? It's so unfair.'

'Be your age,' Bilbow said. 'What's fairness got to do with it? What's fairness got to do with anything in newspapers? Look, answer me one simple question – who'd look prettier grinning at the public from the advertising posters, her or you?'

'They're not giving her that kind of build-up?' Henry said incredulously.

'They are. I heard them talking about it in the features room. They're sending her on a little jaunt round Europe first. "Clovis at Large", they'll call that. Then I expect there'll be Clovis on Men, – no doubt men on Clovis, too, though I don't suppose she'll write about that – and Clovis on Clothes and . . .'

'But she can't write,' Henry said.

'Well, we've got some good subs. They'll give the raw material a little polish.'

Henry slumped into his chair, aghast. 'Whose idea was this?'

'Coughlin's, I believe. He likes having little birds fluttering around him. He likes them to be grateful to him. Gives him a sense of power, I suppose.' Bilbow dipped a ginger biscuit into his tea and sucked it reflectively. 'I think he's a wanker, myself.'

'Bloody hell,' Henry said. 'And he turned me down for the job!'

Bilbow patted him consolingly on the shoulder. 'Never mind, old son. We've just got to face the fact that it's a woman's world.'

5. MARK

At lunch time Henry went to the pub round the corner, there to console himself with a couple of stiff drinks. And after the drinks he went upstairs to the restaurant and the first person he saw there was Coughlin. He was about to leave at once when Coughlin's companion looked up and beckoned to him. 'Henry!'

Henry stared, recognition dawning slowly. 'Good Lord . . .!' He went over and shook hands.

Coughlin said: 'You know each other?' He didn't seem very pleased to see Henry.

'Old chums,' said the other man, and this was more or less true. They had first met ten years ago, when, by coincidence, they joined a weekly paper on the south coast on the same day. A few years later they moved, almost simultaneously, to the *Evening Globe* in London and they had last seen each other two years ago, when, again by coincidence, they left the *Globe* on the same day, Henry to take a better job on the *Journal* and Mark Payne with no job to go to at all, having been fired that very morning for giving general dissatisfaction.

Two years and not a peep from him and now here he was, lunching with the executive editor of the *Journal* and looking marvellous. He was tall and lean, his hair crisp and dark and lightly touched with grey at the temples though he was a year younger than Henry. He wore a suit that made Henry's heart burn with envy – a work of creative genius in midnight-blue silk, at least ninety quid's worth of made-to-measure elegance worn with the casual indifference of one who knew there were two or three more just like it at home.

'Sit down, Henry,' Mark said. 'Have a drink.'

Henry sat down. Coughlin looked for a moment as if he were about to protest but then changed his mind. He appeared, rather astonishingly, to be treating Mark with considerable deference.

'Well,' said Mark, smiling at Henry, 'this is like old times.'

'Isn't it?' said Henry. It wasn't like old times at all. In old times Mark was even more broke than Henry and lunch was a glass of beer and a sandwich at the 'Cheshire Cheese'. In old times, too, it was Henry who led and Mark who followed but now things had changed. An aura of success hung around Mark like a badge of office.

The débris of an enormous steak littered the plate in front of him. A bottle of very good, very expensive wine and the glass from which he had been drinking it had been pushed negligently to one side, though both were at least a third full. At his elbow now was a large ballon of Cognac. A fat Havana cigar smouldered slowly between his fingers.

Coughlin had not eaten so well, or at least not so lavishly. A chicken salad had been his lot, though this was not surprising for he was on a more or less permanent diet. Inside the lean and hungry Coughlin there was a fat and gluttonous Coughlin striving eternally to get out and neither of them had tasted bread or potatoes in years. Nevertheless, each had been given a small treat today. The fat Coughlin was being fed brandy and the thin Coughlin was puffing clumsily but with evident enjoyment on a cigar that was the twin brother of his host's. For that Mark was indeed the host there could be little doubt. His whole attitude proclaimed it.

And that, Henry thought, was something decidedly new. Mark Payne picking up the tab for a fairly costly meal, and business lunches no longer deductible? Well, well, well.

'What'll you drink?' Mark said.

'The wine will do.'

'Is there really some left?' Mark turned the bottle languidly towards him. 'So there is. Sure you won't have a brandy?'

'No thanks.'

The wine was poured and Henry sipped it politely and said

'Cheers' and the others said 'Cheers', too, though Coughlin frowned at him through his glass, darkly.

'Well, Henry,' Coughlin said, 'I expect you'll be wanting to get back to . . .' And then a waitress came up and said: 'Mr Coughlin? Your office wants you, sir, on the phone,' and Coughlin said something staccato under his breath and stood up.

'Sorry about this, Mark.' His smile was almost obsequious. 'Shan't be a minute.'

'Don't hurry.' Mark made an airy gesture of farewell, or perhaps dismissal, and Coughlin went, and when he had gone Mark and Henry exchanged wide, thin smiles and their mouths said 'Great to see you' and 'It's been far too long' and their eyes said nothing.

They had known each other for ten years and for much of that time they had been friends, though not for all of that time. Frequently they had been enemies, for their relationship was punctuated by short, frequent and explosive quarrels. It had been an uneasy kind of relationship altogether, edgy with rivalry.

Mark said: 'How's Sue?'

'Oh, fine.'

'And Timmy? Must be a big boy now?'

'He's four. He's fine. You married yet?'

'No, old boy – too busy.' Mark snapped his fingers twice, hard. Snap, snap. When he had done that he shot his cuffs and three inches of snow white shirt, fastened by heavy gold links, slid down his wrists.

'What at? Publicity or something?'

'Do what? *Pub*licity? Good God, no.' Mark laughed, as if genuinely amused at the preposterousness of the idea, head back, mouth open. Something else was new – he had had his teeth capped. 'TV, old son. Producing, writing. The things I've always wanted to do. It's been hard work these last two years but you can never make it without hard work.' Snap, snap.

'Make what?'

'It,' Mark said, irritably. 'The grade. You know. The top. IT.'

'Oh. And you've made it?'

'I think so.' Mark lowered his eyes modestly and assumed what Henry had always thought of as his sincere expression, which was effected by inhaling deeply through the nose and turning down the corners of the mouth. It went very well with his sincere blue tie of knitted silk and his sincere black-framed glasses. 'Yes, I think I can say that.'

'Tell me all,' Henry said. He took another glass of wine.

'Well, when I left the *Globe* I got in on a training course with Northern TV in Burnley. Ideal set-up. You learn, do a few programmes and make your mistakes out in the sticks, where nobody cares.'

'Funny business, TV,' Henry said. 'Imagine millions of poor bloody viewers sitting there aghast through your first, faltering efforts. Like having a pox doctor's clerk take your appendix out.' He laughed heartily but stopped when he discovered he was laughing alone.

'It wasn't quite like that,' Mark said coldly. 'I wrote and produced my own show. Late-night stuff – interviews, comedy, music, a little satire, current affairs. But only the *real* people on it. You know?' (Snap, snap.) 'The policy makers, men and women of decision – but not the old ones, the same boring round of dreary politicians, Cabinet Ministers, old farts like that. No, no. I went for the younger people, the ones who are going to shape the future in politics, literature, the arts and like that.'

'Good,' Henry said, politely. 'Sounds very nice. Still doing it?'

'No. I've got something bigger and better coming up now. National-Metropolitan TV this time – the full network. Same kind of show, of course, only deeper. A much broader canvas. It starts next week. I'm producing, writing and presenting.'

Henry looked at the suit, the cigar, the brandy and a twinge of envy shot through him. This didn't look like being his day. Everything that happened and everyone he met seemed to be underlining his own growing sense of inadequacy. 'What's it called?' he asked.

'*Future-Tense*'. Snap, snap. Snap, snap. 'Sort of play on words. There's a hyphen, you see. Makes it more meaningful, if you know what I mean.' Not for nothing had Mark been lunching with Coughlin.

'What a rotten title,' Henry said.

'What do you mean?' Mark's tone was decidedly gritty. 'It's a very good title. I thought of it.'

'Oh.' The wine bottle was empty; only the dregs oozed out. Henry put it down and reached, surreptitiously, for Mark's discarded glass. He had just got it in front of him when Mark picked up Coughlin's equally discarded and equally full glass and emptied that into it, too. 'Here, you might as well finish this up.'

'You're too kind.'

'Don't mention it.' Mark leaned back and relit his cigar with a thin gold lighter. 'Want one of these?'

'No thanks,' Henry said, with heavy irony. 'When I've finished up the leftover wine I'll smoke the stub of Coughlin's cigar.'

'Well, please yourself,' Mark said, faintly surprised. 'But you're welcome to a fresh one if you . . .'

'Oh, never mind. What are you doing here with Coughlin anyway?'

'He saw the pilot of the new show last night and it knocked him out. There were a couple of things he wanted to talk over with me – he wants to get an article done on the show, an article about me. Between ourselves, all being well I may be writing a column for the *Journal* pretty soon.'

Henry winced. Him they wouldn't let write lousy features. Mark they offered columns to. A voice within him screamed with impotent rage: 'It isn't fair! It isn't fair!'

'That's nice,' he said, flatly. 'I always knew you'd land on your feet – having first landed on someone else's of course.'

Mark grinned, the boyish grin, modest and full of teeth. 'Not bad. I might use that in the show somewhere. As a matter of fact, I'm looking around for gag writers, fellows with a gift for snappy dialogue. You know. The quick one-line joke.' Snap, snap.

'Why do you keep doing that?' Henry said, irritably.

'What?'

'Snapping your fingers.'

'Oh, that.' Mark gave the sincere look another work-out. 'I don't know. Too much nervous energy, I guess.'

'That's a change. You never had any in the old days.'

'What do you mean? I've always had a great deal of nervous energy. I'm known for it. You need it in TV. I mean, journalism . . . well.' A shrug emphasized the hint of a sneer in his voice. 'That was never really me, you know. I need a challenge – creative work. Not that I'm knocking journalism, you understand. You don't have to tell me it isn't the easy doddle everyone thinks.'

'I'm so glad.'

'You ought to get out, Henry. How old are you now? Thirty-nine?'

'Thirty-five.' The words came out through gritted teeth.

'Are you? Always thought you were older. Well, anyway. Thirty-five. Journalism's no game to be in at thirty-five. You want to get into TV, that's where the future lies.'

'I'll think about it,' Henry said and then Coughlin came back, very apologetic and also rather annoyed at seeing Henry still there.

'Bloody office,' Coughlin said, sitting down. 'Where's my wine gone?'

'He drank it,' Mark said.

'Bloody cheek,' Coughlin said crossly. He reached for the bottle. 'Christ, he's drunk that, too!'

Mark looked at his watch. 'I don't want to hurry you, Greg, but I've got someone picking me up here at three and I think there were still a couple of things you wanted to discuss?'

'Yes.' Coughlin glared pointedly at Henry who, being a sensitive man and not slow to take a hint, stood up saying: 'Nice to see you, Mark. Good luck.'

'Thanks, Henry. And bear that in mind about TV. I could always find you a job on the show, researching or something.'

'That would be very nice,' Henry said tonelessly and left them. He went down to the bar to soothe his ruffled ego with another drink and on the stairs passed a tall, sensational blonde in a pink trouser suit with the word 'Model' practically engraved all over her. He gave her his very best smile but she looked through him and he went on his way, sighing.

Even brainless model girls were walking all over him today.

Fifteen minutes later, as he came out of the Gents. he saw Mark leaving the pub with the model girl wrapped round his arm and Coughlin padding along behind them with a grin of total admiration on his lips.

Henry followed them out, though they didn't seem to notice him. A snatch of conversation came to him as he walked away towards the office. '. . . dinner at the Trat,' Mark was saying. 'then a spot of dancing at Annabel's and breakfast at the Connaught. How's that suit you, darling?'

The model girl said: 'Yes, yes, fine, but for God's sake let's get going. I don't want to be seen hanging around here.' and then the pair of them got into a pale blue Thunderbird and roared off up the street.

Coughlin caught up with Henry at the corner. His cigar still clung wetly to his lips and he seemed in a mellow mood.

'That's the tragedy of journalism,' he said. 'We let people like Mark Payne get away. Fleet Street should have hung on to him.'

'Whatever for?' Henry said, sourly. 'He was a lousy reporter.'

Coughlin gave him a sharp look that would have been a good deal sharper if the cigar smoke hadn't made his eyes water. 'That kind of jealous attitude does no good to anybody. Mark's exactly the kind of man Fleet Street needs. You know where he's going tonight?'

'I heard.'

'There you are then. He's . . . in touch. He represents the modern generation, the liberal, permissive but *concerned* generation that grew up in the Swinging Sixties and is now coming to flower in the mid-seventies. *That's* an idea – I'll get him to do a feature on that: the way his generation is changing society, trace it all back to the Beatles. There's no one on the paper who could write that sort of piece from the inside, do you realize that? We let them all get away, Fleet Street let them get away. They're all in TV now . . .'

'Mark never grew up in the Swinging Sixties,' Henry said. 'He hasn't grown up yet.'

'What?' Coughlin shook his head impatiently, not even hearing this baleful interruption. 'Of course, we'd need a piece to introduce Mark first – the new, meaningful star of TV. I saw his pilot show last night, you know. Brilliant. Hit the mood of the age absolutely. Well, it's not surprising, I suppose. I mean . . . did you see that girl he was with? Archetypal. Today's Girl from head to toe. Any idea who she is?'

Henry shook his head. 'No.' They walked on in silence for twenty yards or so.

'The trouble with our reporters,' Coughlin said, returning to his earlier grievance, 'is they're suburban. They don't *live*. They're not in there, they're not part of the scene, part of these momentously changing times. But a man like Payne now, he's . . .'

Henry held open the door of the *Journal* building and let Coughlin precede him inside. 'Meaningful?' he said.

'Exactly. That's just the word I was looking for. Meaningful – that's what Mark Payne is.'

Henry followed him to the lift, putting his tongue out at Coughlin's brisk, swaggering back.

6. MORGAN

One of the TV companies, more benevolent or perhaps more publicity-conscious than the rest, had set aside within its West End offices a special room for the use of the television reporters of the national press. It had a TV set, a handful of desks, typewriters and telephones and some people actually went there to work.

Late in the afternoon, Henry went there to discover what was going on in the world of television, having been unable to find anything happening at all in any other branch of show business. At that time of day the room was usually full of fairly industrious men, typing and telephoning and moaning about their respective employers. On this occasion, however, there was only one occupant, Morgan Barstow, who was vigilantly guarding his newspaper's interests by reclining in a leather armchair with his feet on a desk while firing paper missiles from an elastic band at the blank face of the TV set.

'Hello, darlin',' he said.

'Hi. Where are the others?'

'Gone to a piss-up at Wembley.' Morgan lifted his feet grudgingly to let Henry go by. 'They'll give us a ring if anything happens that we ought to know about.' He raised one buttock from his chair and broke wind explosively but without embarrassment. 'Get out and walk,' he said. 'I've carried you far enough.'

Henry pushed a pile of publicity handouts to one side and perched himself on a desk. 'Anything doing?'

'Done a piece about a new kids' programme. Here.' He indicated a sheet of typewritten copy. 'Change the intro a bit and you can bung it over to your people.'

'Thanks.' Henry glanced through the half-dozen paragraphs and began to rewrite them in a style more fitting to the *Daily Journal*.

For a little while there was silence in the room, broken only by the intermittent chatter of the typewriter, the ping of the elastic band and the soft thud of another paper pellet hitting the television screen.

'How's your old woman?' Morgan asked suddenly.

Some days nobody asked after Sue at all. Today everybody did. Some days were like that. It was as if the whole world had entered into a conspiracy to remind him every now and then that he would have to do something about his present relationship with his wife.

'She's all right,' Henry said. His voice was sharper than he had intended.

'Hello. Had a row, have you?'

'Not really.' Henry stopped typing and stared pensively out of the window at the tiny courtyard beyond. 'Have you ever thought,' he said, 'how marvellous it would be if you could turn marriage on and off? If you could just wake up one morning and say "I don't feel like being married today" and you weren't and for as long as you felt like it you could be a bachelor again?'

'Yeah,' Morgan said slowly, thinking about it.

'You'd suddenly revert for a day or two – for however long you wanted – to . . . to freedom. You'd have the place to yourself. You'd be able to stay in bed all day or sit in front of the telly or read a book or go and get drunk, or write a sonnet or . . .'

Morgan's eyes gleamed. 'Go out and pull a bird?' he said.

'No!' Henry's idyllic mood ebbed away. 'That's the whole point. It's not just marriage, it's women you'd be getting away from. Every man needs a sabbatical from women. Look, think of all the rows you've ever had. I bet ninety per cent of them have been with or been caused by women. They're an unsettling element. They disrupt your life. It's women as much as marriage itself that drag you down.'

'You *have* had a row with Sue,' Morgan said.

'No,' Henry shook his head impatiently, 'It's nothing to do with Sue personally. I've felt like this for a long time.'

'You're not going the other way, are you?' Morgan asked, watching him curiously. 'You're not going queer?'

'Of course not.'

'Well, I like women,' Morgan said. 'As a matter of fact, I could do horrible things to one right now. There's a little blonde bird I've had my eye on . . .'

'How *do* you get away with it?' Henry had long been intrigued by the way Morgan seemed to lead a perfectly satisfactory double life, maintaining both a wife and an ever-changing string of girl-friends, without ever apparently running into trouble.'You never take your wife anywhere. I've known you six years and I've never met her. I don't think anyone's ever met her, have they?'

'Only one or two,' Morgan said, with great satisfaction. 'Keep her at home, don't I? I never like to mix my home life with my working life.'

'Or your sex life, it would seem,' Henry said dryly.

'I don't know.' Morgan gave the notion serious consideration. 'I get a bit of that at home, too.'

'Yes, but not all of it. God, if Sue thought I was having a bit on the side she'd kill me.'

'Don't let her know, then.'

'*Your* wife must know, surely. I mean, sometimes you stay out all night. She must have a pretty shrewd idea of what's going on.'

'Probably,' Morgan conceded.

'Doesn't she say anything?'

'Has a go at me sometimes.' Morgan was still sprawled in the chair with his feet up but he had stopped playing with the elastic band and his hands were folded comfortably across his stomach.

'And what do you do then?'

'Drag it into bed and give it one, don't I?'

'And that shuts her up?' Henry looked at him with admiration and some incredulity.

'Course it does. That's what women understand. You should try it sometime.'

Henry shook his head. When they were not quarrelling, he and Sue had a perfectly enjoyable and satisfactory sex life, into the spirit of which she entered as enthusiastically as he. But somehow he couldn't see her taking very kindly to anything so primitive as being dragged into bed and given one, especially if she didn't particularly want one at that moment.

'I don't think it would work for me,' he said. He went on with his typing.

'You want to watch it, darlin',' Morgan said. 'Give a woman

half a chance and she won't just drag you down – she'll stamp all over your face. You've got to show them who's boss.'

He heaved himself out of his chair, yawned and stretched. 'Gawd, I'm hungry.'

'Dieting again?'

'Yeah.' Morgan dieted as constantly as Coughlin but the only effect in his case was that he just seemed to get fatter more slowly. 'I think I'll go and buy some sweeties.'

He went out and in the quietness that descended and lasted until his return, Henry finished dictating the rewritten story to the *Journal*. By then it was about five-thirty.

'The boys at Wembley haven't called, have they?' Morgan asked.

'No.'

'Good. Can't be anything doing there then. I'm off.'

'Where?'

'Cocktail party at National-Metropolitan TV. Coming?'

'We've got something on at home. You could drop me off at Baker Street, though.'

'All right.'

Morgan's car was parked in Cavendish Square. It was a Capri, quite new, but like a mobile slum inside, being strewn with bits of paper, old garments and discarded chocolate wrappings. Morgan had a very sweet tooth.

Henry got in the back because the front passenger seat was piled high with old newspapers and magazines, some of them dating back several weeks. By the look of things, on those rare occasions when Morgan did take his wife out she was not permitted to share the front of the car with him.

'What's the party for?' Henry asked.

'This new show Mark Payne's doing.'

Odd, Henry thought, how Mark, too, kept cropping up today. 'I saw him at lunchtime. He seems to be doing pretty well.'

'Can't be bad, can it?' Morgan aimed the car terrifyingly at a tiny gap between two lorries, got through, raised two fingers at the protesting drivers and yelled foul abuse at a pedestrian who had the effrontery to look as if he was about to cross the road.

When this mild uproar had subsided, he said: 'Big mate of yours, isn't he?'

'Who, Mark? He used to be – in a way.'

'Play your cards right and he might row you in on his show.'

'That would be lovely,' Henry said. He was about to expand on this when Morgan created another diversion. He had pulled up at a traffic light and suddenly he yelled: 'Here, look – a Jungle Bunny!'

'Where?' Henry stared around him, though he didn't know what he was looking for because he had no idea what a Jungle Bunny was.

'There!' Morgan pointed, his gleaming eyes and outstretched finger turned in the direction of a slim young black girl who was gazing in the window of a dress shop.

'I thought you didn't like coloured girls,' Henry said.

'Changed my mind, haven't I? Tried one the other night – not bad.' He wound down the passenger window and leaned across. 'Hey, darlin'!'

The Jungle Bunny turned towards them. She was a tall girl with a good and supple figure and there was a sexy grace about her movements. Her hips and buttocks seemed to lead independent existences of their own and jiggled about in a most disturbing way. Her skin was dark, fully negroid, though her features weren't. The lips were full but not thick and high cheekbones gave a lean line to her face. She was very pretty.

'You talking to me?' she said. The lilt of the West Indies was there in her voice but only just. There was a diverting hint of Liverpool, too. She sounded as if she had been working very hard at developing a fashionable and classless English accent.

'Yeah,' Morgan said. 'You doing anything, darlin'?'

'Like what?' The Jungle Bunny leaned against the car and looked in at the occupants with a kind of wary amusement. She was wearing a white skinny sweater and black bell-bottomed corduroy trousers and the skin of her arms was sleek and shiny.

'Want to come to a party?' Morgan asked.

'Where?' she looked from Morgan to Henry and back again without showing any preference for or particular interest in either.

Henry found himself gazing at her rather foolishly and also feeling strangely excited. It was so long since he had picked up a girl that his involvement in this pick-up, vicarious though it was, thrilled him and the fact that the girl was coloured seemed to add extra spice to the situation.

'National-Metropolitan TV,' Morgan said.

'Straight up?' She stared at him sceptically.

'Sure. Here's the invitation.' He took it from his pocket and passed it to her. Behind them a car hooted impatiently and Morgan turned his attention briefly from the girl to lean out of the window and yell: 'Belt up or I'll come back there and hang one on you!' The hooting stopped.

The girl said: 'All right. Why not?' and got in beside Henry.

'Hi,' she said.

'Hi,' said Henry. He was breathing rather quickly, because her knee had brushed against his and the air was sweet with the scent she wore. She had long wide eyes and long, curling eyelashes, cleverly mascaraed, and her lipstick was pale and pink.

'Jamaica?' Morgan asked, all of a sudden.

Feebly, Henry murmured: 'Give me a chance. She's only just got in the car.'

'Quick as a flash and witty with it,' Morgan said.

The Jungle Bunny gave a wan little sigh. The joke apparently was not exactly new to her.

'Barbados,' she said, 'but a long time ago.' Then . . . 'Are you coming to the party, too?' she asked Henry.

'I'm afraid not. I . . .'

'He's going home to his wife and kid,' Morgan said. 'You're all mine, darlin', you lucky girl.' They had stopped at another light and he swivelled round to leer boldly at the Jungle Bunny who gave him a coolly non-committal stare in return. She was plainly a very modern sort of girl who wasn't easily to be impressed by anyone or anything.

It occurred to Henry that he was the third who made the crowd and all at once he wanted to get away. He wasn't excited any more, though he still found the girl attractive and in a curious sort of way he felt protective towards her. There was something vulnerable about her and he was a little uneasy at leaving her with the voracious Morgan. But on the other hand she wasn't his pick-up and it was probably just as well. He had lost the art of chatting up strange birds after all these years.

'I can get out here,' he said. 'The station's only up the road.'

'As you like,' Morgan said.

Henry opened the door and held out his hand to the Jungle Bunny. 'Goodbye. Have a lovely party.'

'Thanks. Nice meeting you.' They shook hands, formally. Her fingers were long and slim and the skin of her palm was a little rough.

Morgan said: 'Hop in the front seat, darlin', and let's be cosy.

You can throw some of this muck in the back.'

Henry walked away towards Baker Street, feeling depressed. There was Morgan off to a party with a good-looking girl. And there was he, off home like a dull and dutiful husband.

Coughlin was right. It was a suburban life Henry led, a soft-centred, soft-scented, female-dominated life. There was no continuity in his existence. It was broken up into well-defined sections – home section here, work section there and it needed an almost physical effort to re-attune himself whenever he switched from one to the other. Most men probably lived that way, ruled by idiots like Coughlin during the day and pretty little dictators like Sue at night, with no time to lead a real life of their own.

It shouldn't be like that. The whole thing should flow, so that work life and social life complemented each other and each was an integral part of a harmonious whole. Mark Payne's life was probably part of a harmonious whole. Mark Payne's life was probably organized that way, Henry thought jealously; a full life, so arranged that each part equipped him for maximum benefit and enjoyment of the other.

He had a sudden, total conviction that he was being left behind, that he was missing out, that somehow or other he wasn't getting his share.

When he had gone a few yards, the car went past him with a great victorious blast of the horn. The Jungle Bunny was kneeling beside Morgan and throwing great piles of paper into the back seat. She smiled and waved at Henry through the rear window as the car made a reckless right hand turn towards Regent's Park.

7. SCENES FROM DOMESTIC LIFE . . . 2

'I remember, I remember . . .'

One of those cold, wet days of winter; not the kind that give English women their smooth, soft complexions but the kind that cause English men to end their days knotted up with rheumatism and arthritis. Rain that would have been monotonous had it not changed occasionally to sleet; a wind that bit with icy teeth; and cold that crept in through the buttonholes of Henry's coat and the pores of his skin and established squatter's rights in his bones.

At two o'clock he was dispatched with all haste to Chelsea to interview a society woman who had been named as co-respondent in a famous divorce case. At 2.30 he knocked on her door to be told by the maid that she was out and would not be back till late.

At 2.35 he telephoned this information to the news desk who told him to 'Hang on there for a bit, old man. The editor's very keen on this story. Doorstep for a while in case she comes back early, old man.'

There was no cafe or pub in which to wait, no friendly doorway to offer shelter. He doorstepped in the rain, leaning against the railings outside the woman's house until he felt conspicuous there and then going to the corner and waiting until the cold made his teeth chatter and then strolling to the other corner where he got just as cold and wet and then walking up and down, up and down, keeping an eye on the house. Nobody arrived.

At five o'clock he phoned the office again. 'No luck, old man? The editor's not going to be pleased. Can't you find out where she is?'

'No, I bloody well can't.'

'Well, just hang on, old man. We'll send you a relief as soon as we can. Must be a bit chilly, hanging around there.'

At seven, he phoned once more. 'Where's that bloody relief?' He was almost crying with cold and anger.

'Won't be long now, old man. He's on his way.' At 7.30 the door of the house opened and the woman, who had been at home the whole afternoon, came out in mink and diamonds and stepped into a taxi, which had just pulled up outside her gate.

Henry said: 'Excuse me, I'm from the *Daily Journal* . . .'

The woman said: 'Go away' and started to close the door.

'I was wondering if I could have a word with you . . .'

'Go *away*.'

The window of the cab was open an inch or two at the top and through this aperture Henry called desperately: 'What we want to know is whether you're going to marry Lord . . .'

The woman, who was about forty and very beautiful, with an Hon. in front of her name and all the advantages of an upper-class background and education, settled herself in the corner of the taxi and said, in her exquisitely modulated voice: 'Don't you understand plain English, you nasty little bastard? Go and pry elsewhere.'

At nine o'clock Henry arrived home, his body stiff and aching, his trousers clinging cold and wet to his legs, his feet awash inside his thin leather shoes and his spirit bruised and bleeding.

The living-room was warm with a coal fire going well. Near the far wall there was a table, a light behind it and Sue sitting at it, typing.

' 'Lo, darling.'

' 'Lo, darling.'

He crossed to her for the ritual kiss of reunion. Her face turned up abstractedly and pink lips brushed against his stubbled cheek. He sighed.

'God, I'm cold. I've never been so cold. I've been hanging around in the rain all afternoon.'

'Ah, shame.' Her fingers moved rapidly across the keyboard as he went to the cupboard and poured himself a stiff shot from the remains of the Christmas whisky. 'God, I'm cold.'

'Still cold out?' she asked.

He gave her a sharp look but she was staring at the paper in her typewriter and before he could say anything she was off again at the rate of about seventy words a minute. Clatter, clatter, clatter – ping: clatter, clatter, clatter – ping.

He pulled a chair close to the fire and sipped his whisky.

'Have a good day, dear?' she said.

'What?'

'Have a good day?'

Another sharp look but she still wasn't watching him. 'Not bad. I got drunk and spewed on the editor's carpet. Then I raped a sixty-year-old secretary and set fire to the managing director.'

'Mmm. That's nice. That's . . . what I . . . like to hear.' Her preoccupied gaze was fixed on what she had just written, while she made corrections with a pencil and her tongue protruded pinkly between her teeth.

Henry sighed again. Louder. No response. He lit a cigarette and fidgeted irritably in his chair.

'What's to eat?'

'Huh?' Her concentration was fiercer than ever. Small white teeth bit into her lower lip.

'I SAID "WHAT'S TO EAT?" '

A quick look up, frowning. 'No need to shout. You'll wake Timmy.'

Pause.

'Well?' Impatiently. 'What's to bloody eat then?'

'Wha . . . ? Oh. I don't know. What do you want?'

'Shit!'

The tempo of the pencil increased, blacking out whole lines and writing substitute versions in the spaces above. 'You'll have to get it yourself then. Do you mind? I must get this finished.'

He found some bacon and eggs and ate them alone in the dinette while Sue, who had eaten with Timmy, went on working. The dirty crockery from her meal was still on the draining board.

'Christ, haven't you even washed up?'

'Huh? Oh, sorry, darling. I've been awfully busy. I was hoping you might do it.'

He did, with the clacking of the typewriter for company. Once he went back to the living-room to complain . . .

'You *still* haven't got that washing up liquid I asked for. You know very well this stuff gives me a rash.'

She looked up, blankly. 'What? Oh, sorry, love. I thought that was the stuff you liked.'

'Well, it isn't.'

'Didn't it?'

He gave up, baffled, and retreated to the kitchen. He seemed to spend a lot of time alone in there in the evenings, cooking and washing up.

When he had finished he returned to the living-room and sat down again. 'I did three-quarters of *The Times* crossword puzzle on the train,' he said rather proudly.

Silence.

He allowed himself another sigh, his third of the evening. ' "Did you really?" ' he said. ' "Yes, I did as a matter of fact". "Well done". "Thanks, I thought it was a pretty good effort".'

Still silence.

'Look,' he said. 'Will you please . . .'

She pulled the paper out of her typewriter and gave him a happy smile. 'That's that, Another chapter finished.'

'Oh, hoorah,' he said, sarcastically. 'Hoorah, hoorah, hoorah! Now do you think you might give me a teeny bit of your attention? Do you think you might deign to exchange the odd civil word with your husband? Or have you some more chores for me? I've done the cooking and I've done the washing up. Perhaps you'd like me to dust the furniture. If you stuck a broom up my backside I could sweep the floor as I went round.'

Quite unfairly, he thought, she took offence at this. 'You resent it don't you? You hate me working at something of my own. You hate me *doing* anything. You hate . . .'

He said, defensively: 'That's untrue, you know it is. I'm all for you writing books. Good Lord, I was the one who encouraged you to do it. All I ask is that you should write them some other time. I don't get many evenings at home and it would be nice if we could just chat a bit occasionally. But every night when I come in you're writing or drawing or mooning about thinking of the next chapter. I don't see why you can't do all this during the day.'

'During the day? *During* the day?' She sprang up, angry and aggressive. 'What on earth do you think I do all day?'

'I don't know but there must be . . .'

'Oh, God. Look, I clean this house all day, I shop all day, I cook all day, I wash and scrub and dust all day. I look after your son all day' – Timmy was always Henry's son, never apparently hers at times like this – 'that's what I do all day. You come in moaning about the tough time you've had and get all nasty because I ask if you'd mind getting yourself a snack, well, what kind of a time do you think I have, stuck here with only Timmy to talk to and the same boring chores to do week in and week out?' She ran to the door, opened it and turned back to him. 'Well, all right. If that's what you want, I'll forget the book. I'll burn it, I'll tear it up. I'll finish with it for ever. I'll just sit here and vegetate and watch *Coronation Street* and waste the tiny little bit of talent I've got and it'll be worth it because I can't stand your mean reproaches any more.'

The tears began before she was out of the room and they were still going on in full flood when Henry found her lying face down on the bed.

'I'm sorry, love,' he said. 'I didn't mean it, honestly . . .'

8. EMANCIPATION

The bungalow was small and nondescript with pink-washed walls and black paint round the windows. A rakish white fence tried, with pathetic lack of success, to give the minimal garden the appearance of a paddock and there was a phoney wishing well on the front lawn.

Henry stopped halfway up the path to look at it.

'Just what we need,' he said. 'A wishing well. No home should be without one. I bet if you looked hard enough you'd find grotty little stone gnomes dotted about.'

'Henry,' Sue said, grittily, 'you will be nice, won't you?'

'I'm always nice.'

The front door was open and sounds of general merriment came from the back of the house. The hall, which was small and bare, had been converted into a buffet-bar for the evening. A table against one wall held an assortment of sandwiches, vol-au-vents with mysterious grey fillings, home-made canapés on brittle toast, cutlery, paper plates and napkins and even a couple of jellies. There was a little flag stuck on each pile of sandwiches to identify the contents: 'Cucumber', 'Cheese', 'Salmon and shrimp'. A powerful smell of fish-paste hung around like body odour.

On another table against another wall stood the drinks – South African sherry, Spanish Chablis and several bottles of allegedly French wine with impressive and unidentifiable labels.

'Look,' Henry said, 'Chateau Soixante-Neuf du Pape.'

'Shut up, Henry.' Sue muttered. She was smiling ever so brightly at their hostess, Lorna Collins, who had just gushed out of the back room to meet them. Henry knew her slightly and disliked her. She was a small, dark, neurotic woman with eyes that shone too brightly and hands that moved too much and intellectual pretensions above her station.

She fell upon Sue with squeaks of joy and the pair of them left faint lipstick marks on each other's cheeks.

'Look everyone,' said Lorna Collins. 'Our guest of honour.'

She dragged Sue, blushing modestly, into the party and Henry sloped along behind, ungreeted and ignored. Someone thrust a glass of harsh yellow wine into his hand and someone else gave him a paper plate and a damp tomato sandwich and he knew at once that it was going to be a ghastly party.

There were about forty people there, most of whom he had met but hardly knew, all crammed into a rather small L-shaped lounge with Sanderson wallpaper and mock-Habitat furniture that was depressing to look at and impossible to sit on.

Most of his fellow-guests gave Henry a nod of welcome and one or two went so far as to say 'Hello'. He returned the greetings perfunctorily and, having deposited the plate and sandwich on a tiny occasional table, leaned against the wall to survey the scene.

The action was at the other end of the room, where Sue had been taken by Lorna Collins and was now surrounded by a gang of women interspersed with one or two husbands. All the local intellectuals were there – people who read the *Guardian* and the *New Statesman* and were left-wing and proud of it and politically ignorant and unaware of it. They wore jeans and open-necked shirts and denim suits ten years too young for them.

A copy of Sue's book, to be published the day after tomorrow, was propped up on the mantelpiece. *Timmy and the Eavoes* she had called it, the Eavoes being a pixie-like race of little people that she had invented. She had done all the illustrations herself and they were very good.

The room was smoky and hot and smelled unpleasantly of food and sweat. Voices rose and fell and blended with each other and collided with each other and drowned each other and odd snatches of admiration shrilled across from the crowd around Sue.

'Darling, you *are* clever!'

'Absolutely brilliant!'

'How*ever* did you manage it?'

'George read it to Sarah and she was *thrilled*!'

Henry went into the hall and got himself another drink. It was cooler there and he drank his wine by the front door, looking out at the twilight. The windows of the neat little suburban houses glowed back at him. Somewhere, over there beyond the park, was his own neat little suburban house where Timmy was tucked up in bed and the baby-sitter was watching television. Henry wished he was with them.

He finished the drink and poured another. It was pretty disgusting stuff but at least it was alcohol. He poured a glass of Spanish rosé and put a slug of sherry in it as a stiffener and went back to the party.

Sue was still hemmed in by her admirers, a different set now but all saying much the same things as the last lot. She looked very pretty in a little black dress that ended around her knees. It occurred to Henry that she had very good legs and it would be nice if they could end their current hostilities tonight in the time-honoured fashion.

She looked up and winked and beckoned to him to join her and he was on the point of doing so when a woman who was passing by stopped in front of him. She had long black hair and jangly ear-rings and bangles on her wrists and she wore a black velvet blouse and an ankle length skirt of the texture of a horse blanket and she said: 'Why, look – it's Henry, the man who holds his tootle.'

Henry said: 'What?'

'Haven't you heard? Oh, it's too funny!' Her voice was like a bark, loud and confident. 'Angela told me all about it. You *must* have heard.'

'I don't know what you're talking about.' Henry strove to keep his tone pleasant but it wasn't easy.

'Angela's little girl was talking to your Timmy at school. Last Monday, I think it was. Or Tuesday? Anyway, it doesn't matter. Well, they were talking about making pi-pi and Angela's little girl said that she always sat down to do it and Timmy said: "My daddy doesn't do that. He stands up and holds his tootle." '

The telling of this rather dismal anecdote was too much for the raconteuse. Tears of mirth rolled down her cheeks and she shook so fiercely that wine spilled out of her glass onto the carpet. Henry watched her bleakly and bled internally with the embarrassment of it.

But one or two people near-by, who had overheard the story,

were laughing too and others, who hadn't, were saying: 'What's so funny? Let's hear the joke', and all of a sudden it was going round the room and everyone was chuckling and looking at Henry. Even Sue smiled until she saw his face and then she stopped smiling and frowned instead.

Henry forced himself to grin. He grinned until the muscles of his cheeks hurt and then he finished his drink and went out to get another and a bearded man standing beside Sue said: 'Going off to hold your tootle, old boy?' and this was too excruciatingly funny for words and the whole crowd howled like dogs.

Henry didn't look back. There was no need to. He could see them all in the mirror in the hall, staring at him, nudging each other, heads thrown back, mouths open and black. Every party needs a butt and he was it. Sue struggled across the room to him . . .

'Henry, I . . .'

'What lovely friends you have. What a lovely matched set of bastards.'

'Darling it was only a joke!'

'I'm glad you enjoyed it.'

'But, darling . . .'

'Oh, get back to your rotten friends!'

And then she vanished into the crowd again for, after all she was the guest of honour, the celebrity, and the others were going to suck her dry. A fresh mob of admirers formed around her and he saw her peering between them, anxious and cross.

He found a half-pint tumbler on the bar and filled it with sherry. It went down like medicine and lay hot on his stomach but it helped. He filled the glass again and took it to the door.

After a while someone came out from the lounge and he thought it might be Sue again. He kept his back turned, waiting for her to approach him, preparing a few angry words to hurl at her. She'd insisted on dragging him to this bloody awful party, after all . . .

Wine slopped into a glass and then a voice behind him said: 'Hello, old chap. Finished holding the tootle, then?'

Henry knew the voice. It belonged to a man called Colin Graves who worked at the town hall and whom normally he quite liked. Tonight, not being normal at all, he said: 'Shut up.'

'Sorry, old man.' Colin joined him at the door and they stood in silence, staring at the night.

'Enjoying the party?' Colin asked.

'Not much.'

'Nor me.'

Henry's desire to go, to walk out and leave the place, drew added strength from the possibility that he might have found someone to go with him. 'Let's nip up the road for a drink,' he said.

Colin smiled wistfully and looked over the brim of his glass of Spanish Sauterne at the chattering mob which, overspilling now from the lounge, was gathering around them.

'Wish I could, old man.'

'Well, come on then,' Henry said, impatiently.

'Don't be daft. There'd be hell to pay when I got home. The little woman . . .'

'Damn the little woman. Who wears the trousers in your house anyway?'

'That's a bloody silly question,' Colin said, irritably. 'You know perfectly well who wears them. The same one who wears them in every home.'

'Not in my house.' Henry shook his head, firmly. '*I* wear the trousers in my house.'

'Big talk,' Colin sneered. 'Go on, then, prove it. *You* go off for a drink. Go and tell your wife you're bored with the party and you're going up to the local. Go on.'

Henry caught sight of Sue in the centre of a predominantly female group across the room. She looked very pretty and very animated and he hated her briefly for enjoying it all. She looked up and saw the scowl on his face and shook her head sadly, as if he were quite hopeless, beyond redemption and unworthy of her sympathy. Her blonde hair swished like a curtain in a breeze.

'I don't want to,' Henry said, sulkily. 'Not on my own.'

The sweet smell of the cheap wine, riding on the breath of Colin's jeering laugh, hit him in the face. 'I bet you don't, old man. I *bet* you don't.'

Momentarily, Henry toyed with the idea of hitting him. It would be a relief and more than that it would be a gesture – a masculine gesture. For he realized now what was really wrong with this party: it was overpoweringly feminine. Woman dominated it. Woman had chosen the time and the place, the food and the wine; probably even the guest list. Men were there as so many accessories, welcomed only because they were joined in marriage to the women who had been invited.

In such a set-up the effect of something definitely masculine, like hitting Colin in the eye, would be stupendous. Very likely not a person present had ever seen a real blow struck in anger. The men had probably forgotten how to fight – if they had ever known – and if they still knew, the women would never let them do it. Fighting was too primitive, too masculine. Women could rarely hope to control a situation where quarrels and arguments were decided by might. That was why they thrived so well in this civilized age; because in a civilized age altercations were settled with words and tears and cold silences and these were women's weapons.

Men like Colin were responsible for this – men who wouldn't even leave a lousy party to go for a drink with a friend because their wives would be cross.

'You're emasculated,' Henry muttered, bitterly. 'You've got no balls, that's your trouble.'

'Oh, drop dead.' Colin walked away to join Sue's group by the window.

Henry topped up his sherry with white wine and looked around for a kindred soul.

A tall, balding man named Gavin Something-or-other came out of the lavatory and paused, staring around in a disenchanted way. Henry sidled over to him.

'Having a lovely time?' he asked.

'No. I hate these affairs.'

'So do I.' Henry offered cigarettes and Gavin, moved by this token of friendship, took one.

'You know why these parties are so terrible, don't you?' Henry said, flicking his lighter.

Gavin nodded. 'Because they insist on serving this bloody awful sherry.'

Jostled by the crowd, they moved back into the lounge, into the centre of the festivities.

'No, no.' Henry waved his cigarette about. 'It's because the women have taken over.' Boosted by the sherry and his sense of grievance, the theory was taking shape nicely in his mind. 'Look, a few years ago men organized the parties. They were the ones who decided. Right, they'd say to their wives, I've got forty people coming to dinner on Saturday – see to it. And their wives would. Or the bloke would say "The Smiths have invited us for seven o'clock tonight. Be ready".'

'Long time ago now,' Gavin said, sadly. 'Victorian times, they were.'

'Maybe. They knew a thing or two, though, those Victorians. We could learn a lot from them.'

'Too late now,' Gavin said. 'Times have changed. Balance of power and all that. Women are the only ones who've got time to organize parties these days. That's why we always get this bloody awful sherry.'

'Right.' Henry was getting quite excited, envisaging himself as the leader of a revolt, a new campaign to return to the days of male dominance. 'So let's do something about it. Let's start putting our feet down. Let's be the boss again. Let's . . .'

' 'Scuse me,' Gavin said. 'My wife's beckoning to me.'

'. . . get our balls back.' But Gavin had gone.

Henry glared balefully after him. Lily-livered bastard. Well, by God, at least there was one man left in this room and he was about to prove it by getting out.

Henry turned determinedly to go and then Sue drifted up and said in a low, cold voice: 'For heaven's sake, try to look cheerful for once.'

And he had just swivelled round to deal with her in his forceful, Victorian way when the woman with the ear-rings and the bangles and the hairy skirt wandered by with a friend and said: 'Ah, there's the man who holds his tootle.'

A lull had fallen over the room and her voice rang out hard and clear. One or two people started to giggle, reluctant to let a good joke die, and everyone turned in Henry's direction again.

He closed his eyes for a second and took a deep breath. Then, turning his head very slowly towards the woman in the hairy skirt, he said: 'Why don't you fuck off?'

9. THE COCKTAIL PARTY

Henry slept alone that night.

There was a brief, violent and not entirely unexpected row on the way home in which phrases like '. . . been so humiliated in all my life' and 'how could you, how *could* you?' and 'God, I hate you sometimes' seemed to recur pretty frequently.

When this had been going on for some time, Henry who, for the most part, had kept a dignified and aloof silence, said: 'I think I did you a favour. You don't need friends like that – they're all bums.'

'Bums? Who are *you* to call *them* bums?'

'I'm not a bum.'

'Huh!' There was a lot of meaning in that brief explosion of breath.

'What do you mean – huh?'

'You know what I mean.'

'I do *not* know what you mean. Explain it to me, please.'

'Work it out for yourself – if you're not too drunk.'

Henry bore this with remarkable fortitude, as he did a nifty passage about thirty-five-year-old adolescents and self-pity that seemed to be getting a little below the belt.

On the whole he felt curiously elated, as if he had indeed struck a blow for male emancipation, and so he kept silent, answering Sue only when it became unavoidable and then as noncommittally as possible.

When they reached their house they smiled and put on bright

faces for the baby sitter and Sue said what a lovely party it had been and Henry said it was just too divine and took the baby-sitter home.

By the time he got back, Sue was already in bed, tucked up in the spare room with the light out and the door closed.

By then, too, Henry's elation – or perhaps just the effect of the drink – had begun to fade and he was feeling guilty. Looked at from Sue's point of view it had been a rotten thing he had done. Remorsefully, he remembered how thrilled and proud she had been that her friends wanted to give her a party. And now he had gone and ruined it.

All right, perhaps they were a dreary and pretentious bunch who had turned up to honour her, but was that really an excuse for hurling four-letter words at a silly woman, even if she did dress like a horse and bark like a dog?

Everyone needed a defensive skin of some kind and theirs was pretentiousness, just as his was . . . what? God only knew. Something, anyway.

And besides, while hurting them was one thing and a perfectly reasonable act, hurting Sue was something else again and had not been at all his intention.

He tapped on the door, opened it and peered into the blackness of the room. 'Sue?' he murmured, contritely, 'I didn't mean . . .'

'Get out,' she said. She sounded as though she might have been crying, though whether the tears had stemmed from grief or rage was hard to tell.

'No, please . . .'

'Get *out*!'

Rage, Henry decided. It must have been rage. He shut the door and went, lonely, to his bed.

Nor were things a great deal better in the morning. Polite, oh yes, she was that. Also silent and ominous.

Breakfast was a grossly uncomfortable meal, not at all improved by the fact that Timmy refused to eat, spilled his milk and insisted on singing 'Jesus, friend of little children' in a flat but piercing voice throughout.

'Leave the table,' Henry told him at last. 'If you can't behave like a human being, shove off.'

Timmy got down, trailing eggshell and breadcrumbs into the lounge.

'Don't take your spite out on the child,' Sue murmured icily.

'I am *not* taking my spite out on the child. If you can't teach him table manners . . .'

'If *I* can't . . .!'

Further hostilities were arrested by the miscreant Timmy, who, putting his head round the door and scowling fiercely, yelled: 'Jesus, friend of little children is here!'

'Good luck to Him,' Henry yelled back. 'If He has to put up with much of your company He won't be a friend of little children very long.'

Timmy scowled some more and searched for a riposte. 'Bloody!' he shouted at length and retired triumphant.

Sue said flatly: 'There's the publisher's party tonight.'

'Am I invited?'

'I suppose so if you don't intend to ruin it.'

'I didn't intend to ruin last night's.'

'You could have fooled me.'

He let that one go by. 'Where is it?'

'The Falcon Club in St James's. Six thirty.'

'I'll be there.'

'All right.' She didn't seem to care much either way.

Henry found his briefcase and made to kiss her goodbye but she averted her face, leaving the kiss stillborn on his puckered lips.

'Sue,' he said. 'I'm sorry.'

'Yes,' she said. 'I know. You always are.'

There was a memo waiting on his desk from Candlish's secretary, and attached to it a large circular invitation in gold pasteboard. The memo said: 'Mr Candlish usually covers the cabaret openings but as he is still away perhaps you would like to go.'

The invitation said: 'The Golden Circle requests the pleasure of your company at the London cabaret début of the sensational Miss Lotty Penny!!!' The date of this breathtaking event was printed at the bottom. Today's date.

Henry took the invitation to the news editor who looked at it in a desultory way and said: 'You might as well go, I suppose. Who is she anyway?'

'A jazz singer,' Henry said casually, having only a moment ago acquired this knowledge from the reference library. 'Pretty good, too. Shall I do a review?'

'Shouldn't think so. It's a small paper tonight, fuck-all advertising. There won't be much space.' The news editor called the entertainments editor on the internal phone and put the problem to him. Afterwards he said: 'No, no review. Just go and have a look at her, see what happens.'

Henry spent the afternoon in the reporters' room at the TV offices. It was quite crowded today since there were no alternative attractions such as piss-ups to entice the regular inhabitants away and everyone was fairly busy, in his own individual way, embellishing and developing small morsels of information handed out by the television P.R.O.s . . .

'How much are you saying that singer's getting from ATV?'

'I don't know. She wouldn't tell me.'

'I know but we've got to *say*'.

'All right, well I'll say a thousand pounds a show.'

'All right, well I'll say nine hundred.'

Henry enjoyed this game. He said £1,150 a show because it was a more impressive sum and, true or false, nobody was likely to deny it. When news came through that the BBC was to televise a forthcoming world championship fight inspiration seized him and he asserted that £23,500 had been paid for the privilege. His masterstroke was to insist that a provincial network was spending one million pounds on a serial about the day-to-day adventures of a village postman.

Soon after six, with no more important announcements from the television scene to report, he made an arrangement to meet Morgan at the Golden Circle at 8.30, washed his hands, combed his hair and took a taxi to St James's.

The location chosen by Sue's publishers for the press reception was a private room belonging to a slightly impoverished gentleman's club, and let off at moderate prices for such occasions as this.

It was oak-panelled and Burgundy-carpeted and sombre oil paintings of nineteenth-century dignitaries frowned portentously from the walls. Wall lights with tasselled shades shone faintly in the dusty gloom and ancient waiters in white coats creaked around dispensing weak drinks and frugal canapés to the assembled guests.

There were about thirty of these guests, book critics and the occasional gossip writer, a percentage of agents and a few men from the publishing house. There were also three authors – Sue and two others – in whose joint honour the festivities were being held.

It was an unusual affair. Parties such as this were normally given only for established writers with a large guaranteed sale who didn't need the publicity anyway. The notion of giving one for a trio of unknowns, or at best little-knowns, with books coming out on the same day was the inspiration of a bright public relations man, who had reckoned that with such a three-way bet there was a fair chance of getting enough newspaper coverage – if not increased book sales – to justify the expense.

When Henry arrived, the guests of honour were grouped bashfully round the fireplace having their photograph taken. They made an odd trio. There was a donnish man of about forty who had written a worthy and rather dull biography of Eleanor Roosevelt's mother· there was a woman of fifty who wrote romantic novels about eighteenth-century heroines with flashing eyes and heaving breasts and there was Sue. looking very pretty indeed in a long black dress. Regarding them objectively, as a newspaperman, Henry was quite certain that she, being the youngest and prettiest, was bound to get the chief share of any publicity the occasion might be given. Oddly enough, the prospect didn't please him much at all.

He took a gin from one of the ancient waiters and watched sourly as a small squad of book critics gathered round the authors. There was not as much gushing going on as there had been the previous night but otherwise the situation was hardly different: Sue at the centre of the action. Henry on the outside looking in.

A strange elderly creature of indeterminate sex and vintage materialized by Henry's side, a glass of sherry clutched in one yellowing hand.

Closer inspection revealed that the gender was, probably masculine since the figure was clothed in an old-fashioned morning coat and a large briar pipe hung from the mouth. What confused the issue was the peculiarly soft feminine quality of the skin and features which, in conjunction with the clothes, gave the impression of a very old male impersonator.

'Good evening,' said this person in a rather high voice.

Henry nodded, curtly. A depression had settled upon him and he was in no mood for social chit-chat.

'Permit me to introduce myself. My name is Edward Sholto.' A thin hand was proffered and perfunctorily shaken by Henry. 'And you, sir?'

Henry introduced himself.

'A writer, sir? Or a critic?'

'Neither. I'm a writer's husband.' There was a surprising degree of bitterness in Henry's voice. 'Susan Copper happens to be my wife.'

'Aha.' Mr Sholto took his pipe from his mouth and wiped a thin stream of spittle from his lower lip and chin. 'I congratulate you, sir. A very promising writer. We have high hopes of Miss Copper.'

We? Oh, but of course. Edward Sholto. Sholto and Coll, Publishers.

The trio of authors had broken up and Sue was now talking to a silver-haired man from one of the Sunday papers and a tall immaculate character in a double-breasted suit, who was both her agent and the man who had rejected Henry's novel. Henry disliked him very much.

'I'd better go and join my wife,' he said.

'Yes, of course.' Mr Sholto was standing directly in Henry's path and made no move to get out of the way. There was a distinct touch of the Ancient Mariner about him and it began to look as if Henry was the one of three that he stoppeth. 'You say you're not a writer yourself, Mr Copper?'

'No and my name's not Copper. It's Tyson,' Henry said shortly.

'Is it?' Mr Sholto remained where he was, peering up and over the bowl of his pipe which seemed far too heavy for his thin jaws. 'Copper's a better name for a writer. Tyson – too ordinary. Susan Copper, yes, good name. She's a very talented young lady. You must be proud of her.'

'Oh, I am, I am.' Henry grinned bleakly at Sue over Mr Sholto's white head.

'Not a writer yourself, eh?'

'That's what I said.' Henry could see no way of escape. He was against the wall in the corner and short of thrusting Mr Sholto forcibly from his path he would have to stay there, at least for the moment.

'Ah, well, we can't all be talented. Talent, like beauty, is a precious gift bestowed on the rare few. The rest of us, the ugly and the ungifted, can only applaud it, humbly, and marvel at those to whom it has been given. Don't you feel that?'

Henry didn't, as a matter of fact, and he didn't much like being lumped along with Mr Sholto among the ugly and the ungifted either.

'I must say,' said Mr Sholto, wiping more dribble from his chin, 'that I admire men like yourself, happy to remain in the background, unsung and unhonoured, while your more talented wives . . .'

'Oh, for God's sake!' Henry said and catching Mr Sholto briefly on the wrong foot, slid past him and plunged across the room to his wife's side.

She kissed him coolly on the cheek and smiled goodbye at the departing book critic. 'You remember Charles Liddell, don't you darling?'

Henry said curtly that he did and he and the agent Liddell shook hands with grim formality and mutual antipathy.

'What a bore that Sholto is,' Henry said, looking back at the old man who was still in the corner peering about him and sucking his pipe.

'Yes. Able man in his day, of course, but a bit doddery now. Arnold Çoll runs the firm these days.' Liddell's voice was loud, clipped and confident, three qualities that Henry particularly loathed in a voice.

Sue put her hand on Henry's arm. Her manner was not unfriendly and it seemed possible that she had almost forgiven him for last night's disaster. 'Darling, marvellous news. George Hackenbauer's in town. He's interested in the book and he wants to meet me.'

Liddell smiled tolerantly upon her. Being taller than Henry and more massively built he rather dwarfed Sue who, despite being quite tall herself, assumed the proportions of a fragile little girl beside him. That was another thing Henry didn't like.

'More than interested, my sweet. The contract is all but signed. Still, George likes to meet the author in person. It gives him a greater sense of involvement. As a matter of fact we're having dinner with him tonight.'

'We?' Henry said.

'Susan and I.'

'Are you indeed?'

'You're invited, too, darling,' Sue said. 'Of course you are.'

'How lovely.'

The look of happy excitement that Sue had been wearing vanished suddenly and the grey of her eyes became the grey of the skies in times of dirty weather. Henry didn't care. He'd had about enough these last two nights.

'Who's George Huggerbugger anyway?' he asked.

'Hackenbauer,' Sue hissed between her teeth.

Liddell sighed the sigh of one confronted with the incurably ignorant. 'He's only one of the five most important publishers in New York, that's all. And he's only going to publish Sue's book in America. And he only believes that she's probably written a children's classic to rank with the work of Beatrix Potter and possibly Kenneth Grahame. And . . .'

Henry clutched at the coat of a passing waiter and relieved him of another drink. 'Well, I can't go to dinner with him anyway. I've got to watch a cabaret at the Golden Circle. I was hoping,' he said to Sue, 'that you'd come with me.'

'Oh.' She looked downcast. 'What time is it?'

'Half-past eight.'

'Couldn't you get there later? Couldn't we have dinner first and then go on?'

'I've got to be there at half-past eight,' Henry said stubbornly, though he knew that the Penny woman would not be doing her act until eleven o'clock at the earliest. He remembered Morgan's words – 'give a woman half a chance and she'll not only drag you down, she'll stamp all over your face.' This was the time for a little masculine dominance, a demonstration of firmness. Anyway, if the contract was practically signed what did Sue have to go and dine with the man for?

'Oh, well,' Sue murmured, dispiritedly, 'in that case we'll have to scrub dinner and . . .'

'Nonsense,' Liddell said. 'It's much more important for you to meet George than to go to this cabaret.'

'Yes, you're right,' Henry said, sighing. 'I'd love to come with you but unfortunately I have to go to the Golden Circle. I know mine's only a menial job but it does help to pay the bills and since Beatrix Potter here is not yet able to support us all . . .'

'Henry!' Sue's voice was shrill with rage. 'That was a rotten thing to say.'

They glared at each other and Liddell stood beside them managing, at the same time, to express sympathy with Sue and disapproval of the cad Henry. It was a lot to get into one expression but he did it.

At that point and before the situation could deteriorate further, Mr Sholto joined the party along with a photographer who said: 'Could I have a picture of you with Mr Sholto, Miss Copper?'

Sue managed a smile. 'Of course.'

She ranged herself on one side of the decrepit old publisher and Henry was about to line up on the other side when Liddell said: 'Not you, old boy. Just the two of them, I think.'

'That's right, Mr Copper,' said the photographer.

'Tyson!' Henry snarled, but nobody was taking any notice of him any more. Sullen and cross he began to back away.

'Give my love to Huggerbauer,' he said.

'Hackenbugg . . . Hackenbauer!' Liddell yelled, furiously.

Henry put his glass down on a table and walked out.

10. THE JUNGLE BUNNY

The Golden Circle was in the basement of an office building near Piccadilly. A doorman in a crumpled uniform guarded the entrance and a tiny lobby festooned with photographs of large-breasted chorus girls with powerful legs and silly faces served as an anteroom to the delights to come. From the lobby a long flight of stairs led down to the club itself, plunging dimly into an atmosphere that was both dank and stuffy. The smell of damp grew stronger with every downward step.

A man with a scarlet dinner-jacket and a troglodyte complexion greeted Henry at the bottom of the stairs and led him through the tight scrum of tables to where the press had been quartered. The place was packed and sweaty and hazy with smoke. The music of a four-piece band fought listlessly against the clatter of crockery and the monkey-house clamour of the customers.

The Press were accommodated at three tables tucked away in an obscure corner of the room. Morgan was there already, yelling abuse at a waiter, from which pursuit he broke off temporarily to wave Henry to the seat opposite him. Henry sat down and Morgan, having done his duty in his self-appointed role as host, turned his attention back to the waiter.

'I said Chambertin, you stupid git!'

'Hello,' said the Jungle Bunny.

Henry had not noticed her in the near-darkness but now he discovered that he was sitting beside her and as he shook her hand he experienced again the excitement he had felt when Morgan picked her up the previous afternoon.

'Are you with Morgan?'

'Well, I was.' She nodded ruefully across the table to where her escort was throwing his arms around the shoulders of a blonde girl in a low-slung dress. Henry couldn't resist a sneaking moment of admiration. The man seemed to draw girls as easily as most people drew breath.

'Where did he find her?'

'I've no idea. She just appeared and he pounced on her.'

'Do you mind?'

'Not much.' The Jungle Bunny eased her chair closer to Henry's and her leg touched his. 'Are you alone?'

'Yes.'

'No wife?'

'No. She couldn't make it.'

'Oh, I'm sorry.'

'Yeah,' he said, flatly. She looked at him with curiosity but asked no more questions, thus revealing a sense of tact for which he was grateful.

Apart from Morgan and the blonde girl, there were two other couples sitting at the table, man and wife in each case, whom Henry knew slightly. He nodded to them and they asked how he was and he said he was fine and he asked how they were and they said they were fine and he said he was glad to hear it and, having revealed himself to be a master of the social graces, helped himself from a bottle of what passed for champagne at the Golden Circle.

'It rather looks as if you're stuck with me,' he said to the Jungle Bunny.

'I don't mind if you don't.'

She was wearing a tiny dress of something white and flimsy, which chastely concealed her breasts but provocatively revealed practically the entire length of her slim black legs. Her lipstick was even paler than it had been the previous day and she was wearing false eyelashes of startling and highly improbable length. Henry thought she looked marvellous.

'I don't mind a bit,' he said.

In fact, he was feeling far more cheerful than he would have thought possible. Until a few minutes ago the latest row with Sue had been worrying him a good deal, had left in him a confused sensation of remorse and indignation. Once again, he had gone a long way towards ruining her big moment. He had been rude to her friends, or at least to her agent; he had been churlish and petulant; he had walked out on her and of all these sins he had repented. But on the other hand, he didn't think she had behaved all that marvellously towards him. Wasn't the blame as much hers as his? Wasn't a wife's place at her husband's side? Damn right it was. Why should he be the one who made sacrifices all the time? What was he supposed to be, anyway, a sort of courtier or pimp hanging around her skirt-tails – if tails were, indeed, what skirts had these days? Wasn't marriage supposed to be a give-and-take affair, and, if it was, was he supposed to do all the giving all the time?

All right, so Sue had written a book and he hadn't. So what? So fine, marvellous, wonderful. She was a clever girl and three rousing cheers for her. And that having been said, did she not owe him something? Wasn't it reasonable to demand that she accompany him to the Golden Circle instead of getting all sulky because he wouldn't go with her to meet the Huggerbugger man? Male emancipation, he said to himself. He had this night struck another blow for male emancipation and as a reward he now found himself sitting beside this black and glossy beauty. Life, he thought, could be fair when it wanted to . . .

'It was a lovely party last night,' said the Jungle Bunny. 'Pity you weren't there.'

'Yes. I thought about you.' He peered at her in the gloom and she gave him a shy little smile and glanced away.

Across the table another row was in progress. With the reckless generosity of one who knew he would not have to pay the bill, Morgan had ordered caviar for himself and the blonde girl but the waiter had vetoed the suggestion.

'Caviar's on the ally cart,' he said. 'The press has the table dote.'

'I'm an invited guest,' Morgan cried, waving his round gold invitation card in the man's face.

'You're only invited to the table dote, not the ally cart,' the waiter said.

'Call the bloody manager!' Morgan was so far incensed as to relinquish his grip on the blonde girl who, deprived of his supporting arm, fell slowly off her chair still gamely crying 'I want caviar' as she disappeared beneath the table.

There was then much bellowing and gesticulating from the outraged Morgan and a great deal of stubbornness on the part of the waiter and Henry, who had rather fancied caviar himself, cravenly decided he'd just as soon have smoked salmon, which, though not quite so exciting, had the advantage of being on the *table d'hôte*.

'Did you hear that?' Morgan demanded, when the waiter had gone. 'Bloody liberty. Well, that's them finished. If they think they're going to get a nice little notice out of me, they can think again.' He looked at the Jungle Bunny. 'You all right, darlin'?'

'Fine, thank you.'

'Good. Henry'll look after you, won't you, Henry?'

'Of course,' Henry said and Morgan, having done his duty by his original guest, turned his attention back to his new one whose lips were open and moist and whose arms, now that she had regained her seat, were entwined around his neck.

In a while, at Morgan's insistence, several bottles of Chambertin arrived on the table, to be followed shortly by the food and shortly after that by the appearance on the tiny stage before them of the six chorus girls whose photographs decorated the foyer and who now went through a clumsily erotic dance routine wearing bits of net and sequins and wide, desperate smiles.

The noise in the place had become so deafening that conversation across the table was practically impossible and Henry discovered that even simple remarks had to be delivered with his lips close to the Jungle Bunny's ear. He did not mind that at all and questioned her closely in this way while the chorus line clumped across the stage and the four-piece band made as much din in the confined space as a full-scale orchestra and the customers played a concerto for knives and forks.

'What do you do?' he shouted into her ear.

'I'm a dancer,' she shouted into his. Her breath was warm and scented on his cheek.

'Where?'

'Nowhere at the moment. I'm resting.' She smiled, showing lots of white teeth. She looked particularly vulnerable and in need of protection when she smiled. 'I do some modelling, too. It keeps me in food and tights.'

The chorus girls went away and the band played old-fashioned tangos and things for a spell. Morgan took the blonde girl onto the dance floor and rubbed his stomach against hers.

'Looks as if you've really lost your escort,' Henry said.

The Jungle Bunny shrugged. 'Easy come, easy go. How about another drink?'

Henry poured more wine and the waiter brought them meringues that tasted like chalk, the lights dimmed and the Golden Circle's resident comedian bounced onto the stage dispensing professional bonhomie.

The humidity in the room had become almost unbearable. Henry's suit was sticking to him and tiny trickles of perspiration were forming on the Jungle Bunny's cheeks and naked shoulders. There was still an hour to go before the long-awaited debut of Lotty Penny.

'Are you writing a notice about this woman?' the Jungle Bunny asked.

Henry shook his head. 'Is she any good?'

A shrug. 'I've heard worse.'

The comedian was saying '. . . and the Earl said "No, Parker, hand me my tweeds. I think I'll smuggle this one into town." ' His friends and relatives at the ringside tables fell about in uncontrollable mirth. The comedian held up his hands to quell the riot of laughter which he appeared to believe was engulfing the entire room. 'No, don't! No, you'll only encourage me. No, ta. Really, no, listen. 'Ere, listen! D'you 'ere about . . .'

Morgan, sweating profusely, was biting the blonde girl's shoulder. The two other couples at the table were huddled close together, holding an intimate four-sided conversation.

'Let's put it this way,' the Jungle Bunny said. 'She's not Ella Fitzgerald exactly.'

Her knee was pressed against Henry's and when she leaned over to talk to him, she rested her hand on his leg.

'I'm glad you're here,' he said.

'I'm glad, too.'

' "! . . . walk this way?" ' the comedian was saying. ' "Look if I could walk that way I wouldn't need talcum powder" '

'God, he's a drag,' said the Jungle Bunny.

'Isn't he?'

They stared at each other, their faces very serious. 'Let's go,' Henry said, suddenly and hoarsely.

He was breathing very quickly and his throat was thick.

'Where to?'

'I don't know.'

'How about my place? It's quite near.'

He hesitated, just for a moment, while the thought of Sue came to his mind. What the hell? Sue didn't need him. He was an embarrassment to her, the party tonight had shown that. She was out now, living it up with the American publisher and that creepy agent, so if he, Henry went off with this sexy black lady, whose fault was it? The situation could never have arisen if Sue had been here, with him where she belonged.

'Yes,' he muttered. 'Let's go there.'

She gathered up her handbag and they stole away. None of the others seemed to notice them go.

It struck Henry as he followed her through the maze of tables in the dim light that this was what Coughlin had meant about the In-Touch people, the liberal generation. A cocktail party, a night club and then off and away with an exotic and beautiful stranger. He felt very proud of himself. He was part of the scene at last.

11. BEDTIME...

The Jungle Bunny's place turned out to be quite a long way off, at the top of a large, rambling house in one of the seedier streets around the Earl's Court Road. There was stained glass in the window of the front door and a square of cardboard in the stained glass. The mat inside the door was badly worn and the lettering on it said 'We-come', which made Henry giggle because he was nervous.

The house was divided into bed-sitters, grandly described as flatlets by the landlord, and the Jungle Bunny said that all the occupants were girls. Henry was not surprised. The place seemed to smell of girls, a sweet-sour smell compounded not only of scent and powder but even, it seemed to him in his present state of terrified excitement, of female flesh.

The Jungle Bunny led the way up the stairs and he struggled along behind her, breathing hard. 'I'm going to commit adultery,' he kept telling himself. 'I'm going to be unfaithful.' And because he had never done any such thing before, he panicked.

For a moment he paused, halfway up the dusty stairs, while a voice which he could only assume belonged to his better nature said 'Get out now – before it's too late!' His body was a battle-ground in which desire and fear grabbed at each other's throats.

And then the Jungle Bunny turned round, frowning. 'Come on,' she hissed. 'What are you waiting for?'

'Nothing. Coming.' And he plugged on after her, inspired by a different kind of fear – the fear of what a fool she would think him if he turned now and bolted out of the house. Her long prette legs twinkled ahead of him, the short skirt bouncing with thy movement of her body, flashes of knicker showing dramatically white against the darkness of her skin.

The Jungle Bunny had rather superior accommodation by the standards of this house, since she occupied not only a bed-sitter but also a miniscule kitchen-cum-bathroom in which the bath was concealed by a hinged wooden top which also served, at non-bathtimes, as a table. The furniture was old and shabby and none too clean and there was a huge damp patch on one wall. Bits of clothing were scattered about the chairs and floor.

Swiftly the Jungle Bunny gathered up some of the débris. 'Sorry. I got up in kind of a hurry.'

Beside the sink there was a dirty coffee cup and a plate with egg fossilizing on the rim.

'Want anything to eat?' the Jungle Bunny asked. 'Drink? There's some beer somewhere.'

'No,' Henry said. 'Nothing. Thank you.' He stood awkwardly by the kitchen door, avoiding her eyes and wondering what he ought to do. He was unused to this kind of business, out of practice and most disconcerted by the offhand way in which she was handling the situation. In his day, all those years ago, pre-Beatles, pre-Permissive Society, girls behaved very differently when he finally succeeded in gaining entry to their bedrooms. In the first place, this latter feat was an immense accomplishment in itself and one which was normally achieved only after considerable groundwork on his part. It hardly ever happened as the result of a casual meeting.

And in the second place, having allowed him in, the girls tended to become giggly and kittenish and there was a good deal of squealing and mock indignation and much cooing of 'Ooh, don't!' and 'What *are* you doing?' and 'Ooh, we shouldn't!' Never, in his recollection, did they behave in this coolly offhand way, almost ignoring his presence, as if it were the most natural thing in the world. Perhaps they were younger, those girls of his youth.

'How old are you?' he asked, suddenly.

She was cleaning her teeth at the sink, brushing vigorously at her mouth as if it belonged to someone else. 'Twenty,' she mumbled through the toothpaste, pink foam frothing on her lips. 'How old are you?'

'Thirty-five.'

'Really?' she sounded indifferent. 'You don't look it.'

Ah, but he felt it. He felt as though he belonged to another age and, in a way, perhaps he did. The difference between him at twenty and her at twenty was a whole generation, a different way of life.

He watched as she washed her face and stripped off the false eyelashes, which she dropped on the grubby windowsill where they lay like sleeping centipedes. With the make-up gone she began to look twenty rather than the twenty-five or so he had assumed her to be.

'Want to wash?' she asked. 'Use my toothbrush?'

He shook his head.

'Right then.' She walked past him into the bed-sitting room. He realized suddenly that he had not even kissed her yet and he wondered whether he ought to grab her and, as it were, crush his lips against hers. But it was so long since he had tried that manoeuvre on anyone except Sue that he doubted whether he could carry it off with any kind of aplomb.

'Unzip me, will you?' she said.

'What? Oh, yes. Right.'

She had her back to him and he grabbed hold of her dress with his ten thumbs and somehow pulled the zip down to where it came to an end in the hollow of her back. With a wriggle that travelled from her neck to her ankles she shrugged the dress off.

'And the bra,' she said.

He found the double hook and eye on the straps and started pulling and tugging at them but succeeded only in digging his fingernail sharply into her skin.

'Ow!' she cried, crossly. 'Do you have to be so clumsy? Oh, leave it! I'll do it.' She twisted round, standing close to him, her hands reaching behind her in that familiar female contortion and as she whipped the brassiere away her breasts fell suddenly into his hands like fat black pears.

'Sorry!' Hastily he let them go.

'Well, go on,' she said. 'Hold them. They're not going to bite you.'

'Oh. OK.' He took them in his hands again and gave them a speculative squeeze.

'Ouch!' she yelled. 'You're not squeezing oranges, for God's sake! What are you – some kind of a sadist?'

'Sorry!' Confused and blushing he stooped with clumsy chivalry to kiss the place and make it well but even as he bent down she was flouncing away from him in great irritation, with the result that her right breast slapped him fiercely across the mouth and the left, following up fast, jabbed him smartly in the eye with its firm nipple.

'Oh, for God's *sake*!' she said, 'What *are* you doing?'

He crouched there miserably, one eye watering and wondered whether to make a run for it. He was too old for this kind of thing, too old and too out of touch.

'Well, come on,' she said. 'Aren't you going to undress?'

When he looked up she was climbing, naked, into the bed. The sheets were grey, crumpled and grubby and he did not fancy them at all. Once, of course, he wouldn't have cared or even noticed. But now he had been married too long. Comfort had become very important to him.

'I . . .'

'Hurry up.'

'Yes. All right.'

He tried to ignore the sheets and looked instead at her. She, at least, was clean. Her skin glistened and she smelled nice. Besides, even without trying to be, she was very seductive, if a little too brisk about it for his liking.

She lay between the sheets, her hands behind her head and watched him undress. He did it clumsily and with acute embarrassment, shielding himself wherever possible with hands or discarded garments. A stripper giving a performance like his would have bored her audience to sleep.

'You're getting fat,' she said. He held his stomach in but it only made the tyre rise higher up his body. Holding his shirt in front of him, he looked down at his pale, thickening torso. Not a sight, he had to admit, to send a woman frantic with desire but even so she might have shown a little more enthusiasm. This was her idea, after all, as much as his. There was no need to be rude.

Dully, he approached the bed and when he got there dropped his shirt and made a dive for the protection of the sheets in one swift, desperate movement.

'Do you always go to bed in your socks?' she asked.

'Blast!'

He stuck his feet out of the bed and removed his socks, revealing the strip of sticking plaster on his instep.

The Jungle Bunny looked at it with mild curiosity. 'What happened there?'

'Cut myself with my razor,' he said.

'On your *foot*? Why ever do you shave your feet?'

Bemused, insulted, remorseful already for the sin he was about to commit, Henry could take no more.

'Why don't you shut up,' he said, 'and let's get on with it?'

Her eyes opened wider with surprise. 'All right. What do you want to do?'

'What do you mean – what do I want to do? What do you suppose we're here for? Good Lord, can I possibly have misinterpreted the situation?'

'Oh, a comedian! How lovely. I mean, how do you want to go about it?' She sat up beside him, showing more interest in the technical problems of method and position than in Henry himself.

'What?' He had grown uncertain again. 'Oh, I don't know. Anything you like. I'm sort of . . . conventional.'

She sighed. 'I see. Like mummy and daddy do it. All right, then. Come on.'

She got down under the sheet and pounced upon him and there ensued a brief coupling which, while it brought about the desired end, seemed to him to be otherwise wholly unsatisfactory. She carried out her part of the proceedings with great efficiency but a complete lack of passion, with the result that Henry felt a regrettable absence of involvement. Were it not for her physical presence and its effect, he might as well have been on his own. She went about the matter as though she were performing a minor operation upon him.

'Did you enjoy that?' she asked, when it was over.

Henry considered the question and in his reply politeness won out over strict honesty. 'Yes. Quite.'

'Good. I thought it wasn't bad.' They might have been discussing a film they had watched together. 'You're very quick, aren't you?'

'What do you mean?' he asked, bridling. 'I've never had any complaints before.'

'Well, I expect not.' She sat up with her arms around her knees. Unlike Henry, who lay under the covers with the sheet tucked up to his chin, she had no self-consciousness about her naked body, which, after all, was a very nice body, a bit lean perhaps, but very supple and feline. 'Your wife must be used to it, I suppose.'

'Not only my wife,' he said meaningly, and lying by implication.

She laughed; a mocking sound. 'You mean they're all used to it? Your entire harem? Oh, I can see them now, all your mistresses, having a chat about you over tea – "Old Henry? Well, of course, he may not be good but he's quick." '

There were times when he could dislike this girl. She was too damn confident, that was the trouble. He looked at her dark, glossy back. What right had she got to be so damn confident?

'I mean, nobody ever complained,' he said, angrily.

She glanced at him over her shoulder. The whites of her eyes, he noticed for the first time, were not really white at all. They were rather dark, a yellowish-brownish colour. 'You haven't slept with another girl since you were married, have you?'

'How do you know?'

'I could tell. I don't mind, though.'

'Good of you,' he muttered.

'I'm rather glad, really. It's much nicer. Just like seducing a virgin, in a way.'

This was positively embarrassing. Him, a virgin! After all the girls he had known. He thought about them, their faces flashing across his memory like a series of late 1950s and early 60s pin-ups and after he got to Sue the screen went blank. That was the lot. How many? Four, five? God, was that all? Four or five?

'How many men have you had?' he asked.

She lay back beside him and laughed. She had the kind of hearty, childlike laugh that he had always associated with West Indians. It reminded him of the picture he had formed of her that first day in Morgan's car as a pretty and rather simple girl from the colonies. Boy, had he been wrong.

'Why do men always ask that kind of question?' she said. 'You know, like it was cricket and you had to keep a count on the scoreboard? I've been with lots of men. Why not? Does it matter?'

'No. I suppose not.'

'You always want to be the first, don't you? Like climbing Everest. Well, bad luck.'

'Look, I'm not . . .'

'And why should men always be the seducers?' She brushed his interruption aside. 'You always say, "Oh, I went out and pulled a bird last night". Well, why shouldn't a bird go out and pull you for a change? You enjoyed it, didn't you?'

'What do you mean?'

'You think it was your idea to come up here? Listen, if I hadn't wanted it you wouldn't have come. So you didn't pull me – I pulled you.'

'I see.' My God, he thought, the world had changed more than he had realized. 'Are all the girls like you, these days?'

'I don't know,' she said, impatiently. 'Who cares?'

'But...'

'Oh, be quiet. We didn't come here to talk.' And then her arms were around him again and it was nearly three o'clock when he finally got up and dressed and went home.

12. . . . AND AFTER

What have I done, he thought, Lord, what have I done?

Sunlight filtered through the curtains, dusty and bright, to spread itself in a pool on the pink eiderdown.

Henry turned over, pressing his face into the pillow, though it was not the light he wished to avoid.

Breakfast sounds and smells drifted up to him where he lay, in the spare bedroom to which he had gone when, at four o'clock, he crept into a house that was dark and still and creaking a little in its sleep.

He had felt exhilarated then; a man of the world. The dawn was not far off and he had stood at his front door, breathing in the sweet night air and admiring himself as the kind of man who got home just ahead of the milk and fresh from his mistress's bed.

But that was at four o'clock and now it was half-past eight and the world was different.

What have I done? What have I done?

He was unclean. Loathsome. Despicable. The kind of man who went sniffing around after other women like a randy dog. He hated himself and he hated the Jungle Bunny and he loved Sue and Timmy and his little suburban house with its bright décor and carpets and furniture and its clean sheets.

A spasm of remorse shook him. Those other sheets . . . those other, grey and grubby sheets. God, how could he? How *could* he have done it?

He got up and ran into the bathroom

The water from the shower was hot but not hot enough. He wanted it hot enough to sterilize him the way a surgeon's knife was sterilized. So hot that it would wash away not just his sweat but the smell of the Jungle Bunny and those grey sheets and all the other men who had lain where he had lain last night.

Lain? No, laid. Laid, where he had laid last night. Laid, that was the word. Laid, laid, laid.

He got out of the bath, pink and scalded and still dirty. Sue, I'm sorry. I'm so sorry . . .

The face in the mirror hadn't changed. Heavy-eyed, perhaps, but no mark of sin indelibly inscribed on it. There should have been. The word 'Adulterer' should have been emblazoned across his forehead in great, burning letters.

He looked at the razor in his hand, the edge of thin blue steel glinting as the sunlight caught it. He carried it to his throat, hesitated. No, not that. Not today. Suicide wasn't the answer. The problem was too serious for that.

Memories, powerful, unbidden. The tatty furniture, the dirty kitchen, the crumpled bed, the blackness of her skin, the whiteness of his. God, what if she was . . . What if he had caught something?

Panic now. Don't think about it. How long did it take to show – ten days, six weeks? How long? Forget about it. It was too terrible to contemplate. The sin was bad enough, crushing enough, without that kind of possibility, too.

Prayers. Hands together, eyes screwed tight. Dear God, forgive me this time and I'll never do it again. I promise you I'll never do it again, only forgive me this time . . .

'Daddy! DADdy!' Timmy was at the door, blond, blue-eyed, angelic and hideously betrayed by the one man who should never have betrayed him. Timmy, I'm sorry. I'm so sorry . . .

'Breakfast is ready, Daddy.'

Henry grabbed him up, pressed the soft little body against him. Tears came into his eyes as he stroked the small, blond head. He shook them away with cold self-contempt. This was maudlin. Come on, pull yourself together. Remorse was one thing and he deserved to suffer that. But don't wallow in it. Don't, for Pete's sake, start enjoying it . . .

He dressed quickly, Timmy prattling beside him.

'Daddy, Daddy, do burglars have long noses?'

'What? Well, some burglars do, some burglars don't.'

'Why?'

'I don't know. That's just the way it is with burglars.' He didn't want to go downstairs. He didn't want to face Sue.

'Daddy, come ON! Breakfast is ready.'

'Yeah, right. Coming.'

They went down, holding hands.

Sue at the kitchen sink, wearing a white jumper and an orange skirt, long-legged and . . . clean. 'Hello, poppet.' He kissed her on the cheek but she made no response.

The bacon and eggs were on the plate and the coffee percolator had just had its orgasm. The scent of Blue Mountain filled the room.

Henry sat down at the table and started to eat.

'Cross with me?' She didn't answer. Okay, so she was cross with him. Well, she had a right to be. He shouldn't have left her last night. God, if only he hadn't left her last night . . .

'Have a nice time last night?'

'Yes, thank you.'

'What time did you get home?'

She still didn't look at him. Everything about her, the angle of her head, the set of her shoulders, the tone of her voice radiated coldness. 'About twelve. And you?'

'Oh, I don't know. Threeish. How did you get on? Is Hackenbauer going to take the book?'

'I think so.' Sue turned wiping her hands on her apron, her expression hard and bitter. Henry had never seen her quite like that before and it shocked him that a face so pretty could wear a look so ugly. 'Timmy, go upstairs and wash your face, darling.'

'But, Mummy . . .'

'Timmy!'

'Yes, Mummy.'

When the boy had gone Sue came to the table and sat opposte her husband. She had a cup of coffee and, unusual for her so early in the day, a cigarette.

'What was that singer like?' she asked.

'Oh, not bad. She's not Ella Fitzgerald, you know.' (Where had he heard that before?)

'Did you write anything?'

'No. Well, they didn't want a review in the end, so I just watched her, had a couple of drinks with the boys and came home.'

He was uncomfortably aware that she was staring at him in an unblinking and most disconcerting way. She was also nodding her head, slowly, as if her most awful fears had been confirmed. Henry lit a cigarette, anything to keep his hands busy, to give an appearance of nonchalance and she watched him go through the whole business from producing the packet to sighing out the first drag of smoke and putting the spent match in the ashtray.

Then she stood up, slowly, and smoothed her skirt down with her hands.

'You're a liar,' she said quietly.

'I beg your pardon?' The suddenness of it took him quite by surprise and he could only bluster. A feeling of dark unreality closed in upon him.

'You're a liar,' she said again. 'Look.'

From behind her she produced the morning papers, four of them, and spread them out on the table, threw them rather as if they were a hand of giant playing cards. It was a histrionic gesture but it didn't look rehearsed and the way the papers fell, neatly folded with the top halves of the front pages uppermost, was a chance in a hundred.

'Oh, my God!' Henry said. The headlines gazed up at him, black as doom. SINGER STORMS OUT . . . ROW AT NIGHT-CLUB . . . MISS PENNY REGRETS . . . Only the *Daily Journal* had nothing about it at all. 'What happened?'

He grabbed up the nearest paper – Morgan's – and glanced through it. A picture of Lotty Penny, leaving the Golden Circle and looking angry. And then the story: backstage row five minutes before she was due on . . . dispute over money . . . quotes from her – 'I won't go on'; quotes from the manager – 'I'll sue' . . . quotes from irate customers . . .

'Oh, my God!' Henry said again.

'You weren't there, were you?' Sue said.

'Yes, I was. Honestly.' He couldn't keep the quiver from his voice nor the panic from his heart.

'You're a liar.'

'Well, I . . . Well, I popped out – early. And . . .'

'Where did you go?'

'I . . .' Oh, God, where? He couldn't think. He couldn't think. 'I went out with . . . I went out to . . .' Where could he have gone? At that time of the night where could he have *gone*? There must be places. For God's sake – think.

Sue nodded. 'You were with a woman,' she said flatly. 'Who was she?'

'Sue . . .'

'Who was she?' She stood with her hands hanging limply by her sides and there was nothing in her voice and nothing in her face. A zombie.

'Sue . . . Darling, forgive me. It wasn't planned . . . I just . . . it just happened. Believe me, it was the first . . . I'll never do it again . . . I couldn't . . .' Sounds, words babbling from him; his voice quaking; tears of sorrow and panic blurring his vision.

'I see,' she said.

He was conscious of small, irrelevant things – the brightness of the gingham curtains behind her; the cleanness of the kitchen and the dinette; the way the sun shone on her pale blonde hair. 'Sue, darling . . .'

'I see,' she said and then she turned and went out. He got up and followed her, still making sounds, still letting words stream from him incoherently. The feeling of unreality had deepened into total confusion. Madness must be like this.

Sue was in the hall, helping Timmy on with his coat. Henry stopped.

'Where are you going?'

'I'm taking Timmy to school and then I'm going shopping.'

'But you can't. We've got to talk.'

She ignored him. 'Kiss Daddy goodbye, Timmy.'

Timmy ran to him and Henry caught the boy up in his arms and hugged him as if one of them were certain to drop dead before the day was out.

'Daddy, are burglars little people – little like this?' He held thumb and forefinger about two inches apart.

'Yes. Just like that.' Henry stared at Sue and she stared back blankly. 'We've got to talk, Sue. I've got to explain.'

She shrugged. 'Come on, Timmy.'

And then she was gone.

C

13. TROUBLE WITH COUGHLIN

'I want to talk to you,' Coughlin said – snarled was a more accurate description. 'Come into the lavatory.'

'All right,' Henry said. He had known for some while that Coughlin wanted to talk to him. The news editor had said so.

'Tyson!' The news editor had bellowed as soon as Henry appeared in the reporters' room. 'Come here!'

Henry had gone, warily. It was always a bad sign when the news editor called you by your surname. It meant he was displeased and the only consolation to be gleaned was that he was unlikely to make any jokes. Sometimes Henry thought that, on balance, the man's wrath was more appealing than his humour.

'Coughlin wants to see you,' the news editor said, glaring at him. The assembled acolytes glared, too, backing up their master like some seedy old Greek chorus. 'I think we all know why.'

He nodded grimly at no one in particular and the chorus nodded with him.

'Yes,' Henry said. 'We all know why. I'll go and find him.'

'Bloody fool,' said the news editor to his departing back, 'missing a story like that.'

Henry ignored him. Indeed, he hardly noticed him. All the way to the office the thought of the trouble he was likely to be in over missing the Lotty Penny story had overshadowed his quarrel with Sue but now that he was here the situation had reversed. Worry about Sue made all his other problems seem negligible.

He found Coughlin, a man of regular habits, making his midmorning visit to the executive lavatory and they went in together.

'Well, what have you got to say?' Coughlin asked. He stood in the corner stall, legs apart, head thrown back, hands resting on hips with almost arrogant self-confidence. He was quite a virtuoso in his own way.

'I'm sorry,' Henry said.

'What kind of an answer is that?' Coughlin glanced angrily back at him over his shoulder. It was a dangerous thing to do in the circumstances.

'Mind your shoes!' Henry said.

'What? Oh.' Coughlin removed his hands from his hips and resumed control of operations. 'I'm glad you can take the matter so lightly,' he said with deep sarcasm. 'I wish I could share your attitude.'

'Look, I know I missed the story and I'm sorry, but I don't honestly see what else I can say.'

'Dereliction of duty,' Coughlin said. 'You could be fired for that. You were ordered to be there last night.'

'Well, no. I was told I might as well go along there. It's not quite the same thing.'

'It's exactly the same thing,' Coughlin said.

'But...'

'You're arguing with me again. You're always bloody well arguing with me. I don't like it, I don't like anybody arguing with me. All I want to know is whether you've got a reasonable explanation for last night. Were you ill? Did your car break down? Eh? Anything like that happen?'

'No,' Henry said. 'Nothing like that. I went there and because I knew the paper didn't want a review I left early. That's all.'

'That's all? That's all?' Coughlin was working himself up into a spurious rage. He was very good at that, particularly when he could not, for the moment, think of any more constructive line of action. 'Well, we'll see about that, by God. Get out! But don't think you've heard the last of this. There's no room on this paper for people who don't . . . who can't . . . Get out!'

Henry went, without any great sense of regret. He found himself as strangely unmoved by Coughlin's rage as he had been by the news editor's displeasure. His concern now was for Sue and how he could atone for his infidelity.

He slammed the door behind him and loitered in the passageway, thinking about his problems. When he had been standing there for a minute or two he heard the click of the door handle. He was about to walk on to avoid meeting Coughlin again when, from behind the door, there came an exasperated grunt and the handle began to rattle up and down. When this stopped there was another grunt and the sound of fingers scrabbling at the lock. Then that stopped too, and the next development was the sound of insistent knocking from the inside and Coughlin's voice calling urgently: 'I say! Is anyone there? The door's stuck. Is anyone there?'

Henry looked at the door. The handle was agitating again. 'No,' he shouted.

There was silence for a moment. Then . . . 'I say!' Coughlin said. 'Who's that?'

Henry began to steal away but he had not gone far when the editor appeared round the bend in the passage, his head bent over a sheaf of papers in his hand. An encounter with him was not at all to be desired at the moment and Henry took the only evasive action that offered itself. He opened the door of the nearest office and ducked inside. It was empty. He crouched in the corner and waited.

Through the frosted glass panel he could dimly see the editor go by and stop outside the executive lavatory, just as Coughlin's plaintive cry arose again. 'I say! Who's there? I say!'

The editor put his key in the lock, and gave the door a firm push and Coughlin came out.

'Oh, it's you,' the editor said. 'What on earth are you doing?'

'Tyson locked me in,' Coughlin said.

There was a pause. 'Did he?' the editor said. Another pause. 'I think there's something I ought to make clear to you. I'm all for informality in the office. It's good. You can't run a newspaper on too tight discipline. But I will not have my executives and staff running around all day locking each other in lavatories. It's an unhealthy situation to say the least.'

'I don't understand,' Coughlin said.

'Never mind. I just don't want this kind of thing happening again, that's all.'

Henry sat down on the office floor and turned scarlet with silent mirth. When he had recovered, Coughlin was saying: 'I'm having a lot of trouble with Tyson. His approach isn't contemporary enough.'

Henry hugged himself. Coughlin had got it wrong. He couldn't even remember his own jargon. He had said contemporary when he meant meaningful.

Then his eye caught the date clock on the wall and he made a mental apology to the man. July 1. The month had changed and with it the word.

'What *are* you talking about?' the editor said.

It was the worst question he could have asked for Coughlin was none too sure either. Nobody had ever asked him to define his words before.

'I mean his work's soft,' he said, hurriedly. 'There's no meaning to it, in the sense that it's not meaningful. It's not compulsive . . .'

'I don't understand these terms,' the editor said. 'Besides, he's not Hemingway, you know. He's only a reporter. You can't expect Nobel Prize-winning literature from him.'

Coughlin changed his direction of attack. 'Well, no, of course not. You're quite right. Perhaps I do tend to overanalyse. But then he doesn't seem to be a very good reporter, either. That Lotty Penny story, it was Tyson who missed it, you know. He was at the Golden Circle but he left early.'

'So I gather. To tell you the truth, I'm not sorry we missed that story. It smells of publicity stunt to me. The club's been losing money for months and the singer's a long way over the hill. We can do very well without that kind of story in the *Journal*.'

Coughlin's hesitation was almost imperceptible. 'Ah, you thought that, too, did you? Well, of course, it was the first thing that occurred to me. As soon as I looked at the *Express* this morning, I thought "Hello, someone's pulled a crafty stunt here." Mind you, it was remiss of Tyson . . .'

'Do you think we could discuss this later? I was just on my way to . . .'

'Ah, of course. Yes.'

The editor went into the lavatory and Coughlin, after a moment's indecision, rejected the idea of following him and bustled away down the corridor.

Henry gave him a couple of minutes to get clear and was about to leave his sanctuary when the literary editor came in.

'Hello,' he said. 'Looking for me?'

'Er . . . yes. Yes, I was looking for you but you weren't here.'

'No. I was in the features room.'

'Ah.' With some desperation Henry wondered what reason he could possibly give for wanting to see the literary editor but he was saved the necessity of inventing something when the man said: 'Well, I can guess why you're here. I'll show it to you in a second. Just hang on.'

Mystified, Henry waited while the literary editor crossed the room to where a row of galley proofs hung on hooks along the wall.

'Won't keep you a minute,' he said. 'I'm looking for a short story. We're running one a day next week – well I suppose you knew that. Bloody headache it is, too.'

He riffled quickly through the proofs, casting a quick eye over each and clucking exasperatedly with his tongue.

'Nothing,' he said. 'Would you believe it? Nothing at all.'

'None of them any good?' Henry asked sympathetically.

'What? Oh, I dunno. I expect some of them are all right. That's not the point, is it?'

'I don't know. I don't even know what you're looking for exactly.'

'It's perfectly simple. I'm looking for a short story nineteen inches long but do you think I can find one? Eighteen inches, oh yes, I've got three of those and several 24 inches – very popular length that, for some reason. But nineteen inches – nothing. Believe me, if you could write short stories nineteen inches long you'd make a fortune. Excuse me.'

He picked up the house phone and dialled an extension number. 'No, I'm sorry. I just haven't got anything that length. Would a twenty-four be all right? You could always cut five inches out, nobody would ever notice. Or an eighteen? I've got three eighteens. They might stretch with a bit of leading out . . . No, how should I know what they're about? Does it matter? . . . Well, they're all detective stories, I think . . . Yes, okay, I'll send one up.' He put the phone down. 'Bloody features editor,' he said.

He took down one of the galley proofs, wrote 'Features Ed.' in thick black pencil across the top and put it in his out-tray.

'Now then. This is what you want, I think.'

From his in-tray he produced a page proof and beckoned to Henry to approach and look at it.

It was really quite impressive – half a page devoted to a picture of Sue looking very fetching, and a review of her book, a most favourable review so far as Henry could tell from a quick look at it.

'All right?' said the literary editor.

'Yes. Fine.' Sue. God, what was he going to do about Sue? He had not forgotten her, not for a moment all day had he forgotten her, but in the last half hour she had been eased into the back of his mind. 'It's lovely,' Henry said.

'Yes. Well, she's a clever girl. Young Jennifer Clovis did the notice. I think you owe her a drink.'

Henry thought about Jennifer Clovis, a lanky sort of girl with waist-length hair and a petulant mouth. Damned if he was going to buy her a drink. 'Yes, I do,' he said. 'Excuse me.' He went out.

Somehow his guilt feelings towards Sue had just given way, in a small measure, to irritation. It was always the same, everyone telling him how clever she was, and now the whole business had got so out of hand that the people who thought her clever were getting other clever girls to write clever reviews of his clever wife's clever book. Where would it all end? That's what he wanted to know.

He rang Sue at home but there was no reply and while he was wondering where she might be, the news editor called him.

'Tyson!'

Still out of favour, he noted. He went into the glass-walled office. Coughlin was in there, too, and so was Jennifer Clovis, sitting on the edge of the desk with her skirt hitched up and her eyelashes raising a draught. Judged only by her face she was rather an ordinary sort of girl, not plain exactly but not very pretty either. Nobody, however, judged Clovis by her face, for nature had granted her a truly splendid figure – insolent breasts and a narrow waist, soft round hips and a bottom like an apple and this whole delicious superstructure was underpinned by a pair of long, magnificent legs. She was aware of her assets and her liabilities and therefore ignored the commands of trendy fashion. Caftans and woollies and lengthy, shapeless dresses did nothing for her and she had no dealings with them. Instead, she wore the shortest skirts ever seen since the mini was a uniform and thus drew masculine attention away from the slight vapidity of her face to the firm and fruity promise of her thighs where such attention rightly belonged. Coughlin was now looking at those thighs and making slight chewing motions with his mouth. Neither he nor Clovis acknowledged Henry, though the latter was aware of a thin glance coming sideways at him like a pair of needles from Coughlin's direction.

The news editor thrust a slip of paper into Henry's hand.

'Savoy. 4.30. Press call for some comedian that's landed a big TV series. Take a photographer.'

'All right.'

'About that Golden Circle story . . .' said the news editor grimly. Henry glanced at Coughlin who was apparently taking no interest in the proceedings, but who, for some reason – lust, possibly – had just taken Jennifer Clovis by the upper arm and was kneading her gently.

'Oh, well,' Henry said, 'that was just a publicity stunt, wasn't it? As a matter of fact, as soon as I looked at the *Express* this morning, I thought "Hello, someone's pulled a crafty stunt here!" '

Coughlin let go of the Clovis. His face was turning red and when he looked up his eyes bulged with hate.

'You're not paid to think,' he said. 'You're paid to report the facts. There are people here better qualified than you to decide what's a publicity stunt and what isn't.'

'Well, yes, but this was a pretty obvious one, as I'm sure you'd be the first to agree . . .'

'Never mind whether I agree or not!' Coughlin roared. He was leaning across Jennifer Clovis, the news editor and the desk and his great red face was only inches away from Henry's less great and paler one. 'What I want to know is why the hell you weren't there last night to tell us it was a stunt!'

'Ah, yes,' Henry said, conceding the point. There was a part of him that stood outside himself and marvelled at the coolness with which he was marching, eyes open, into peril. He knew perfectly well that it was dangerous to bait Coughlin like this and he didn't care. He might later perhaps, but not now. 'Still, in this case it didn't matter in the long run, did it?'

'By God . . .' Coughlin said. 'By God . . .' His face and throat muscles were working madly and he didn't seem able to say any more.

'Listen . . .' said the news editor. The previous exchanges had baffled him rather, largely because nobody had yet bothered to inform him of the editor's views on the Golden Circle story. All he knew was that there was some kind of conflict going on between Coughlin and Henry and being a shrewd man with the instincts of the born survivor he knew where his allegiance lay. 'Listen, Tyson, who the hell says it was a publicity stunt anyway? If you want my opinion . . .'

'Of course it was a publicity stunt,' said Coughlin. 'Any fool could see that.'

'Quite,' said Henry.

'I know it was a publicity stunt!' said the news editor. 'Get out!'

Henry went. He stopped at the door and had another look at the paper the news editor had given him. 'How do you want me to do this story?' he asked.

'I don't care,' said the news editor, 'just so long as it's meaningful.' He glanced up at Coughlin, seeking approval.

'Meaningful?' Henry mused. 'I dunno. I was thinking of making it . . . well, contemporary.' He didn't look at Coughlin but he was pretty sure the man's eyes were still bulging.

When Henry got back to his desk, Bilbow said: 'You been getting up Coughlin's nose again?' There was little in the office that escaped him.

'Looks like it.'

'What have you done to annoy him?'

'Nothing really,' Henry shrugged. 'I locked him in the lavatory this morning.'

Bilbow's eyes narrowed reflectively behind his glasses. 'Yes, that might have done it, I suppose. He wouldn't like that much.'

'No. He didn't seem to.'

'Well, take care. He's after the editor's job and with his pull he'll probably get it. Nasty man to cross.'

'I know.'

'Look out,' said Bilbow. 'Here he comes.'

Henry kept his head down, staring earnestly at a TV magazine on his desk, as Coughlin loomed up and stopped in front of him.

'Watch it,' Coughlin said, softly. 'Just watch it.'

A minute or two later . . .

'I don't want to be quoted on this,' said Bilbow, 'but I shouldn't be at all suprised if you'd pushed him just a wee bit too far.'

14. HOME, SWEET HOME

'Bloody fine mate you are,' Henry said. The words were muffled, for his mouth was full of bread and cucumber at the time.

'Me? What about you, then? Only went off with me bird, that's all.' Morgan exuded indignation and finely masticated peanuts, the latter spraying from his lips like machine-gun fire.

Henry wiped the pieces from his suit. 'Well, you did have another one. It wasn't as if I'd left you without a spare. There was that blonde . . .'

'Dropped in the sticky and smelly, did you?' Morgan asked with a degree of satisfaction. His desertion by Henry and the Jungle Bunny the previous night clearly rankled still.

'I did when I got to the office this morning. You might have let me know when that Lotty Penny story broke. I was the only one who missed it.'

They had finished interviewing the comedian who had landed the television series and now they were applying themselves to the serious business of consuming the TV company's gin.

Morgan said: 'I couldn't find you, could I? I mean, when it all started happening last night you'd scarpered.'

'You knew where I'd gone.'

'Yeah, but I didn't know the phone number. I didn't even know if she was on the phone.' Morgan finished his drink, staring at Henry over the rim of the glass with narrowed eyes. 'Not like you to go off with a bird. All right, was she?'

'You should know,' Henry said, sharply.

'Yeah. Well, I thought she was all right. Very lively. You seeing her again?'

'No.' Henry had made the decision as soon as he woke up that morning and the fact that he had been unable to contact Sue on the phone all day only reinforced it.

'What made you go off with her?' Morgan asked.

'Oh, lots of reasons.'

They stepped courteously aside as a large TV starlet in a see-through shirt jiggled by. Morgan followed her progress with eyes that gleamed with gin and lust.

'Wouldn't mind getting my leg across that,' he said. Henry said nothing. He'd gone off sex that day.

Morgan sighed deeply as the starlet surrendered herself to the welcoming embrace of a very small TV producer who vanished into the opulence of her body like one trying to get back into the womb.

'Not like you, that, going off with a bird,' Morgan said again.

'No.'

'I mean, I always thought you were just a looker, not a doer.'

'Yes.'

Morgan said, exasperatedly: 'All right then, don't bloody tell me about it.'

'I don't want to. It was just something that happened that's all. I'm not particularly proud of it.'

'Christ!' Morgan jeered. He was at least two large gins ahead of Henry and it was beginning to show. 'Full of remorse now, aren't you? Talk about the English taking their pleasures sadly.'

'I don't know what you mean.'

'Look, darlin', if you're going to have a bit on the side you might as well enjoy it. There's no point otherwise. *Did* you enjoy it?'

'At the time, yes.'

'Then that's all that matters. Why wear a hair shirt all day just because you've had a bit of grumble?'

Henry stopped a waiter and exchanged his empty glass for a full one. 'It's not easy to trot around with a song on your lips when your marriage looks like breaking up,' he said, gloomily.

'Sue find out, did she?' Morgan made sympathetic clucking noises. 'Well, that's always the gamble, isn't it? It's the risk you take when you go around laying other birds. If your old woman finds out you can't expect her to be too pleased. Carry on a lot, did she?'

'No, that's the trouble. It would have been better if she had.' Henry remembered the breakfast time scene and Sue's remarkable frozen calm. There had been something final about her attitude, as if she had already decided what she was going to do and he wondered uneasily what that could be. In fact, wondering made him so uneasy that he put his glass down and said: 'I'm going home.'

'Yeah, well, you got to face the music some time. Might as well do it now. Good luck.'

Morgan watched Henry's progress through little groups of people to the door and then a thought occurred to him. 'Hey! I might have another go at that Jungle Bunny. What's her phone number?'

Too late. Henry had gone. Morgan shook his head and accepted another drink. One for the road and then – what? Home. Not a cheery thought. He'd not been there for two nights and his wife was always a bit cool when he turned up again after an absence like that.

He took a sip of his drink and looked around him. The small TV producer had gone and the large TV starlet was standing alone beside the window. Morgan sidled up to her.

'Hello, darlin',' he said and mentally he had already got his leg across her.

The house was dark and empty, like something that had died. No Sue, no Timmy – just neatly-made beds, well-polished furniture and carpets briskly swept. Lifeless. This morning it had been a home. Now it was just a nicely furnished house.

Sue had taken most of her clothes and Timmy's too, but the car was still in the garage and she had left her set of keys on the kitchen table. There was no note but then there was no need for one. Henry did not have to be told why she had gone and he could guess where she had gone.

What to do, what to do?

He sat in an armchair and wondered. It was too early to feel shock or regret and he could admit to no surprise, for he had expected something like this. Yet he ought to react somehow, to register something.

Unconsciously he sought refuge in the cliché reactions. What did men do on the movies in this kind of situation? They rushed from room to room, calling the names of the departed. Well, he'd done that.

They lit cigarettes. Henry already had one going.

They had a drink. He had looked for one but there was nothing in the house except a bottle of home-made nettle wine that someone had given him at Christmas time and he didn't fancy that.

So he sat there and he didn't feel shock or regret or surprise. He felt nothing; empty – like the house, and inadequate. He couldn't cope, that was his trouble. He couldn't cope with his job and he couldn't cope with his marriage. He couldn't cope with his ambitions or his frustrations or his limitations. He couldn't cope with the age in which he lived. He couldn't cope with anything. Other men, Morgan for instance, or Mark Payne, hurled themselves joyously into the life of their time and everything came up roses.

He, Henry, had one tentative dabble in it and came up covered in . . . sweet violets.

After a while he switched on the light and went to the telephone and dialled a Surbiton number.

His father-in-law answered the phone. 'Hello, is that you, Henry?'

'Yes. Is Sue there?'

'No, lad, she's not.'

He frowned. 'She's not been there at all?'

'Oh, aye. She's been here. She's staying here. Turned up this morning with young Timmy.' Hesitation at the Surbiton end. 'I gather you've had a bit of a row or something.'

'Something like that. Where . . .'

'It must have been quite a row for Sue to leave home like that. Never done that before, has she?' A soft, north country voice, worried but not unfriendly.

'No. Whe . . .'

'Oh, well, if you don't want to tell me, lad . . .'

'I'd rather not at the moment.' Why did every bastard he met want to be his confidant all of a sudden? 'Where is Sue now?'

More hesitation in Surbiton. 'Well, she's . . . she's gone out. With a feller, like.'

'What? Who?'

'Well, I think it was her agent bloke. She phoned him when she got here and then he phoned her and then she went out, oh a couple of hours ago.'

'Where did they go? Did she say?'

'No. I know she was going up to London. Well, it's all right, I suppose. Leaving Timmy, like. I mean, he's all right with his granny and me. Fast asleep now he is, but . . .'

Henry put the receiver down. He was reacting now, okay, registering splendidly. Anger. Jealousy. Fear.

Good God, was it possible? Could Sue do that – walk out on him and go straight to another man, *that* man? Surely not. And yet . . .

Yes, it was possible.

She could. She had.

He grabbed her car keys from the table and ran out of the house.

15. THE JUDO EXPERT

When he got to Baker Street he parked beside a telephone kiosk and looked up the address he wanted in the L–R directory. A block of flats, South Kensington way.

On an impulse he dialled the number, heart beating like a big bass drum. It rang, rang again, rang, rang again. Then the receiver was lifted at the other end and the telephone gave out its shrill, greedy cry, demanding to be fed money. Henry hung up. His hands were shaking and if he didn't look pale – which he probably did, though there was no way of telling, someone having thoughtfully stolen the glass from the kiosk mirror – he certainly felt pale.

So they were there, at *his* place. By God, wasn't that just like a woman? One lousy, little quarrel and she was off, snuggling down in some other man's bed.

One chance, that was all a woman would give you. Step out of line once, just once, and she was away, inspired by the desire to prove yet again and once and for all that what was sauce for the gander would do very nicely for the goose, too, thank you very much.

He got back into his car and headed south. He no longer felt worried about Sue, nor guilty about what he had done to her. He had sinned, yes, and he was big enough to admit it, but – and this was the point – Sue had sinned more recently than he. First, she had left him and then she had gone off with another man, thus not only wiping out Henry's crime but substituting one of her own in its place.

Dramatically, the roles had changed and now he was the wronged party.

A rich variety of emotions struggled within him for precedence. Jealousy, rage, self-pity – they were all in there, locked together in grim combat like well-matched wrestlers, first one uppermost, then another.

'The bitch!' Henry said as he got to Piccadilly.

'That bastard! I'll kill him,' he said, as he sped past Harrods.

'Sue! Oh, Sue how could you?' he moaned, as he turned left at the lights; 'The bitch,' as he turned right at the next lot and 'That bastard!' as he pulled up outside the block of flats where, according to the telephone directory, Charles Liddell. Litry Agt. had his residence.

It was a tall, thin block with a smug air of prosperity about it. Henry rammed the car savagely into a parking slot that said 'Residents Only', ripped the keys from the ignition, took the pavement in one stride, the steps in another and entered the foyer at a run.

The lift. Where the hell was the lift? No, not the lift. Nobody took the lift in a situation like this. The stairs. Where the hell were the stairs then?

He found them, tucked away discreetly round the corner and pounded up them. Flat 447, 447, 447. He kept the number whirling feverishly around his mind as if he were afraid that if he forgot it for a moment he would forget it for ever.

The first floor? No, not here. The second? No. The third? No. Christ, it must be all the way up on the fourth . . .

By the time he reached the landing his thigh muscles had tied themselves in knots and the breath was burning his throat but his anger was still with him, strong and hot, and pausing only to take on fresh air he hurled himself at the door of Flat 447 and hammered upon it.

'Open up!' he said in a loud pant.

For a moment – nothing. Then within the flat a door opened, a man's voice said something, a woman laughed, the door closed, there were footsteps on the tiled floor and then the main door opened and Charles Liddell was standing there wearing, of all things, that indispensable part of a seducer's wardrobe, a smoking jacket.

'Good eve . . .' he began but Henry brushed the formalities aside along with Liddell himself. With one sweep of the arm he had the door fully open and before Liddell could do anything about it, he was in the flat.

'Where is she?' he said.

Liddell shut the door. He looked amazed. 'What?' he said. 'Who?'

'My wife,' Henry yelled. 'Where's my wife?'

In the mirror behind the door he caught a glimpse of himself, hair tousled, face red, eyes bulging and even as he stood there, shaking with rage, a part of his mind knew he was playing it all wrong. He should have been icy and sophisticated about it, dangerously calm, instead of charging around in this undignified way...

'Your *wife*?' Liddell said.

'Yes, my wife! Where is she! Come on, where is she?'

'I don't know what you're talking about,' Liddell said. He had retreated against the wall and was watching Henry warily. 'Who are you anyw . . . ? Good God! It's Copper.'

'Tyson,' Henry snarled. 'My name is Tyson and my wife's name is Tyson, too, and where the hell is she?'

He glared madly about. The hall was small and white-walled, a Matisse print here, a poster from a Frankfurt Book Fair of long ago there. Doors confronted him on every side, all identical. Which way to turn, that was the problem. He chose a door at random.

'Here!' he said. 'She's in here, isn't she?'

He grabbed the handle, turned it, wrenched it and plunged into total darkness. His foot clattered wildly against a metal dustpan; a broom, disturbed by the violence of his entry, fell off its hook on the wall and smote him across the head. The waxy, lavender smell of floor polish invaded his nostrils. He groped at the broom and knocked the vacuum cleaner onto his foot, fumbled at the vacuum cleaner and kicked the dustpan again. Tins and cans and dusters fell about his person. A whole army of cleaning equipment seemed to have risen up in fury against him.

Behind him there was a short, derisive laugh.

Panicking, attacked on all sides, Henry lashed out against the mindless savagery of his assailants. There was a crash of glass and a thick liquid, violet-scented, white and nasty, trickled down his trouser leg.

Then, suddenly it was over. The brooms and the mops and the Hoovers fell defeated into a corner, the door slammed and Henry, battered but still game, staggered back into the hall.

'Do you want to have a go at the larder?' Liddell said. 'I don't think there's anything in there that'll put up much of a fight.' He appeared to have gathered a good deal of confidence from the preceding farce and the sneer he was now bestowing upon Henry was quite insufferably superior.

Henry refused to suffer it. Humiliation and its stable mate, frustration, had served only to increase his anger and so he gave forth a throaty roar and sprang.

'Keep off!' Liddell cried, hoarsely. 'I warn you, keep off!' He began retreating round the hall, going fast, but backwards, in search of sanctuary but before he could find it, the umbrella stand clobbered him behind the knees and brought him down. He fell and lay yelling while Henry stood above him, fists clenched, glowering and sufficiently bemused by all that had happened as to be unsure what to do next.

And while the pair of them froze temporarily in these positions, one of the other doors opened and a woman came out. She was a pale blonde, quite tall, wearing a green silk trouser suit and Henry had never seen her before in his life.

'What in God's name is going on here?' she demanded.

Liddell answered her plaintively from the floor. 'This maniac's looking for his wife,' he said.

'I'm looking for my wife,' said Henry.

'Well, does he have to make so much noise about it?'

'Don't ask me, ask him,' Liddell said.

'Yes, I do!' Henry shouted, defiantly. 'I'll make all the bloody noise I want!'

Liddell had struggled to his feet and was leaning against the wall, holding his leg and moaning.

The woman said: 'Can't he go and look for her somewhere else?' She addressed all her questions to Liddell, as if she had decided at a very early stage that no sense was possibly to be gleaned from Henry.

'He thinks she's here.'

'I know she's here!'

'Good Lord!' The woman began to laugh, 'Poor man.' She turned resolutely to face Henry, in the manner of one who had decided that this task, distasteful though it was, clearly had to be tackled some time and sooner was better than later and spoke to him slowly and clearly, as to an idiot. 'Look, your wife isn't here. Please take my word for it. She's . . . not . . . here.'

'I don't believe you,' Henry said. 'I'm going to have a look' and he started towards the door from which the woman had emerged.

'Charles,' she said, sharply. 'Are you going to permit this?'

'Oh,' Liddell said. 'Well . . .' He seemed rather wary of Henry again, as if on reflection, the latter's brief but victorious struggle against the contents of the broom cupboard had impressed him as to his fighting qualities.

'Well?' said the woman, 'Don't you think this has gone quite far enough?'

'Ah,' Liddell said. 'Yes. I mean . . . look here . . .'

The woman stood, slender and belligerent, in Henry's path.

'Kindly move out of my way, madam,' Henry said. 'I intend to search this flat.'

'Don't you dare touch me,' she said.

'Don't you dare touch her,' said Liddell. He had armed himself with an umbrella and the possession of it appeared to have lent him courage. He took a step forward, brandishing the makeshift weapon menacingly.

Henry looked at them, ranged indignantly against him and for a moment he was aghast at his own temerity. It was, after all, a bit much, bursting into someone's place like this. His anger started to waver and weaken.

'Well,' he said. 'I . . .'

'Get out!' said the woman.

'Get out *at once*!' said Liddell, adding a neat touch of his own.

Anger rose again and drew strength from their wrath. 'Don't you shout at me,' Henry said.

He whipped round to face Liddell and then, so fast he hardly knew what was happening, the woman grabbed him by the arm and yanked him against her. Her hipbone dug sharply into his thigh, she gave a wrench and a twist and suddenly Henry somersaulted through the air and made a three point landing on hands, feet and backside near the front door.

When he got up, dazed and utterly bewildered, she did it again.

When he rose once more she did it a third time, only now the front door was open and he finished up outside, on his back, on the landing and this time he didn't bother to get up. There seemed little point. He was much too dazed to put up any kind of resistance and if she threw him again the only way he could go from here was straight down the stairwell and he didn't fancy that.

The front door closed with a brisk, triumphant sound and through it and the buzzing in his ears, he heard Liddell say in tones of awed admiration: 'My God, I never knew you could do that. Where on earth did you learn it?'

'GLC judo classes, darling,' the woman said. 'Of course, one really learns it to ward off rapists but it's very effective against other maniacs, too. Let's go and have a drink and you can tell me what it was all about . . .'

Footsteps receded across the hall, an inner door opened and closed and then there was silence.

Henry gave a deep sigh and deemed it safe at last to get up.

16. THE PUKING CAT

The swing doors of the tall, thin block of flats revolved gingerly upon their axis and a very old man hobbled out. He walked with a limp because he had knocked his knee against the banisters on the landing. He walked bent because he had jarred his back on the tiled floor of the hall and he winced with every step because the Amazon in the flat upstairs appeared to have pulled his right shoulder irrevocably from its socket.

But these, the old man thought as he shuffled slowly down the steps, were but minor wounds. The really grave injury was the compound fracture of his self-respect and that didn't show.

He leaned heavily against his car while the cool night breeze brought a little comfort to his aching head, and stared up at the fourth-floor flat with loathing and awe.

What a fighter! Of course, she had taken gross advantage of her sex, being no doubt confident that Henry was not the kind of bloke to slug it out, toe to toe, with a blonde in a trouser suit. Had she been a man, now . . .

Had she been a man, he reflected gloomily, it would probably have been even worse. A man would have thrown him harder, quicker and a great deal more often. Just as well it was a woman, really, otherwise he'd be a stretcher case by now.

God, what a night!

Mind you, if he had been the sort of man who looked determinedly on the bright side of everything, there was, he knew, some consolation to be derived from recent events. Liddell might easily have called the police and had him arrested.

Henry shivered. That would really have been humiliating. Bursting, in the heat of the moment, into someone's flat, demanding to know the whereabouts of one's wife was one thing. Hearing about it the following morning in a magistrate's court was something else again.

'. . . I then proceeded to Flat 447 where I found the accused' – the rustle of notes and the flat, unaccented tones of the policeman's witness-box drawl – 'emerging from the broom cupboard crying "Where is my wife? Where is she? . . ." '

Yes, by heaven, where is she? If not with Liddell, then with whom? He couldn't imagine. He couldn't even think who her friends were. Perhaps she didn't have any.

When he got right down to it, perhaps neither of them had any friends. Plenty of acquaintances, yes; muckers and mates of one sort or another – but not real friends, of the kind one could turn to in times of marital stress.

The sadness of it struck him hard. He had not realized until now quite how close he and Sue had always been. He had had his job and her. She had had her book and him. And they had both had Timmy and that was it. A tight little triangular island, that was what they were – until one corner of it, Henry, went drifting off into the mainstream of people around them.

Why on earth had he done it? What on earth was he trying to prove? And what on earth was he going to do now?

It was madness, a nightmare, to be standing here in the depths of Kensington, battered and sore, wondering where his wife was and with nowhere to go except a house that was empty with a special, desolate kind of emptiness. If he could only turn the clock back twenty-four hours. If he could only be given one more chance . . .

'Hello,' said the Jungle Bunny.

He had not seen or heard her approach but she was standing beside him now, glossy and pretty in the trouser outfit she had worn the first day he met her.

'Hello,' he said.

She surveyed him gravely. 'You don't look very well.'

'I don't feel very well.'

'You've got some sticky white stuff on your trousers.'

'I know.'

'It doesn't look very nice.'

'No, it doesn't, does it?' He dabbed at it with his handkerchief, groaning as pain stabbed him in the shoulder.

'Have you had an accident?'

'Sort of. It's nothing much.'

There was silence while Henry rubbed his trousers and the Jungle Bunny leaned against the car.

'What are you doing here?' she asked.

He hesitated. 'I've been visiting someone. That's where I had the accident.'

'I've been visiting, too. A girl-friend. I was just on my way home when I saw you.' She paused. 'I suppose you're going home, too?'

'No.' He was surprised to hear himself say that. He had not meant to say it but having said it he knew it was true. He didn't want to go home, not unless Sue was there. 'Excuse me a minute,' he said and hobbled across the road towards a telephone booth.

Perhaps that was it. Perhaps Sue had gone home after all. The thought induced a definite lightening of the spirit. If Sue were at home, then he would go home, too, and they could talk and make everything all right again . . .

The number rang and rang and nobody answered. He clicked the receiver rest to get the dialling tone again and rang the Surbiton number. His father-in-law came on.

'Is Sue there?'

'No, lad, she's not.'

He felt panic as well as hurt. Where could she be at this hour of the night? Why was she doing this to him?

'Well, she's not with her agent either. Where the hell is she?'

'I'm sorry, lad, I don't know . . . Look, I hope it's not anything serious. Between Sue and yourself, I mean. I'm not asking, you understand. Sue didn't tell us and I don't suppose you want to either. But I hope it's nothing serious . . .'

'It's serious,' Henry said, curtly. 'It gets more bloody serious all the time. Listen, I suppose you *are* expecting her back tonight?'

A breath drawn sharply in Surbiton was clearly audible in Kensington. 'Well, of course we are. I hope you're not suggesting that our Sue is the kind of girl to go off for the night, just like that, leaving Timmy and not telling anyone where she's going. Well, I'm surprised at you, Henry. Things must have come to a pretty pass if . . .'

'No,' Henry said, 'I'm not suggesting anything. I'd just like to know where she is, that's all . . . How *is* Timmy, anyway?'

'Oh, he's fine. Sleeping like an angel, bless him.'

'Yes, well, give him a kiss for me when he wakes up, will you?' Oh, Timmy, my Timmy, what have I done to you?

'Aye, I will . . . Henry, are you going to be calling again? I mean, I'm only asking because it *is* after eleven you know, and mother and me are early birds. Up early and bed early. You see, I could leave a note for Sue asking her to call you or . . .'

'No. No, don't bother. I'll call again tomorrow. Good night.'

Henry went back to his car. The Jungle Bunny had got into the passenger seat and was sitting with her feet up on the dashboard and her chin resting on her knees. She looked as if she belonged there and maybe she did. Nobody else seemed to belong there any more.

'Well?' she said.

He took a long, deep breath and let it out slowly. 'I'm hungry,' he said, 'and I need a drink.'

'What about the Puking Cat?' she said.

'Do what?'

'The Puking Cat. It's a restaurant. And a sort of disco. It's ever so nice.'

'It doesn't sound very nice,' Henry said.

'Well, it's the latest place. All the pop stars go there.'

'Sounds like a very good reason to stay away.'

'Oh, well,' she said crossly. She seemed to have taken it as read that if he was going for a drink and a meal she was going with him and he really couldn't think of any good reason for contradicting this assumption. 'If you want to be square about it . . .'

'No. No, we'll go to the Puking Cat.'

The time for being square was long gone, buried back in the days when he was a respectable married man. There was no point in it now.

She made a gentle, contented noise. 'Good,' she said. 'The food's lovely.'

The Puking Cat was to be found, inevitably, in the King's Road, Chelsea, and equally inevitably it occupied a basement, a long, narrow room with onions and Chianti bottles hanging from the walls. Outside a neon sign showed a black cat with its back arched and its mouth open, spewing forth a great shower of sparks as if it had inadvertently swallowed a Roman Candle along with its ration of Whiskas.

Inside the light was dim and purple. The waitresses wore tight, white T-shirts and tight, white trousers with a vomiting cat's head embroidered on each buttock and breast. The food was London-Italian and rotten and the music was loud and worse.

Henry ordered tagliatelli and a carafe of Chianti and the Jungle Bunny said: 'Don't you think this place is gorgeous?'

'Yes,' Henry said. 'Gorgeous.' He tried to put conviction into the words but it wasn't a great success. Squareness obviously was not something to be sloughed off like last year's skin or yesterday's happy marriage. Squareness it appeared was a state of mind, a whole attitude to life and such things were not easily changed.

'There's Beethoven!' said the Jungle Bunny delightedly.

'Who?' said Henry, startled.

'Beethoven. Beethoven O'Rourke.' She was waving with great vigour in the direction of a somewhat shambling youth wearing long hair and the jacket of an eighteenth-century army captain. The youth waved back with practised languor. 'He was at number one in the charts last week. Listen, they're playing his record.'

So they were. Somewhere in the dark corners of the room there were speakers and from it now came a song with which Henry was vaguely familiar and which seemed to consist largely of a lot of grunting and the oft-repeated refrain: 'I'm comin', baby, I'm comin'.'

'Beethoven O'Rourke, for Christ's sake!' he said.

He pushed the half-eaten tagliatelli to one side and drank deeply of his Chianti. Coming to the Puking Cat had not really been a great success. He'd have been a lot happier in some decent little Italian place in Soho where he could see what he was eating and the tables and chairs were not so low and the room was not so crowded that every time a dancer went by his head disappeared up her skirt. There might possibly be, he admitted reasonably, a time to put your head up a skirt but not when you were eating tagliatelli.

'Feeling better?' asked the Jungle Bunny. She had drunk little of the wine but she had eaten her food with enormous appetite and now she was finishing his. It was strange, Henry thought, how slim girls always seemed to eat like navvies.

'Yes,' he said. The Chianti had done him some good, anyway.

Mark Payne loomed up out of the darkness and sat in the vacant chair across the table from them. 'Hi,' he said, snapping his fingers.

'Oh. Hello,' Henry said without much warmth.

'I was just across the room talking to Beethoven,' Mark said, 'and I thought it was you, sitting over here. Hard to tell in this light.'

'Yeah, it was me.' Henry said..

Mark was looking marvellous in a four-button double-breasted jacket that had ninety quid practically inscribed on it. God knows what his trousers had cost. Or his shoes, or his shirt, come to that. Henry's entire ensemble had not been worth more than fifty pounds brand-new.

He said: 'I'd better introduce you. This is Mark Payne and . . .'

'We've met,' Mark said.

'Oh ? When ?' A little twinge of jealousy added itself to his other aches and pains.

'At my reception the other night. You know, at National-Metropolitan TV.'

'That's right,' said the Jungle Bunny, looking pleased that Mark had remembered her.

'You came with (snap, snap), don't tell me (snap, snap) – Morgan Barstow. Right ?'

'Right,' said the Jungle Bunny.

'I never forget a face,' Mark said.

God dammit, said Henry to himself. Mark Payne and his almost tangible aura of success were all he had needed to complete the ruin of his night.

The Jungle Bunny got up and excused herself and went away, undulating nicely, in the direction of the powder-room. The two men watched her go.

'Hey,' said Mark, 'where's Sue ? And what are you doing out with a chick like that ?' He leaned across the table, eyes glinting behind his sincere glasses.

'It's a long and sordid story,' Henry said wearily, 'and I don't think I feel like going into it right now. How are things with you ?'

'Oh, great, great.' Snap, snap. 'I think the show is really going to be something. But really.' He put on the sincere expression. 'People around the studios say it could even be better than anything David Frost has done.'

'I'll make a point of watching.'

'I'd like you to and I'd like to hear any ideas you may have afterwards. I meant that about using you sometime.'

'Thanks.' Henry drank some more Chianti, letting the liquor bite into his stomach while the iron burned into his soul.

'I may see you around tomorrow,' Mark said. 'Greg Coughlin wants me to call into his office and sign a contract. It's only a hundred quid a week but a regular column is good publicity.'

Henry was silent. Only a hundred quid a week! Only a hundred . . . A sense of failure attacked him from all directions and he was still sitting there in a state of gloom, reflecting on the unfairness of life, when the Jungle Bunny returned and Mark took her off to dance.

Henry watched them. The Jungle Bunny moved in a boneless, weightless way and Mark was good, too. A little flashy, of course, but as smooth on his feet as he was on his backside.

The hell with him, Henry thought and turned his attention to the rest of the room.

The clientele consisted mostly of thick-lipped pop-singers and bony models on whose sharp flanks a man could come to grief like a ship on rocks. In dress, the men and women were almost indistinguishable, got up in the latest fashions like true devotees of St Carnaby and All Gear.

This, Henry thought sourly, was living. This was the life. Coughlin would be very impressed if he could see him now among all these meaningful, contemporary people.

Gone, gone, the suburban life, the sherry parties, the commuter trains. He was free at last to take his rightful place as a paid-up member of the trendy, trendy, go-go-go Permissive Society.

His head ached and his back was still sore. The room was so dark he could hardly see, so noisy he could hardly hear, so richly perfumed by smoke and scent and sweat he could hardly breathe.

He wanted to go to bed.

Mark brought the Jungle Bunny back. His progress across the room was slow for he seemed to find it essential to pause every few paces and hail, or be hailed by, another pop-singer. With every additional 'Hi!' or 'Hey, there!' or 'How you doin', man?' he seemed to increase in stature, his smile grew broader and sincerity streamed from his glasses like sunlight.

He gave a courtly bow to the Jungle Bunny and tried to ease her into the seat beside him but she carried on walking round the table and went back to Henry. Rather to his surprise she turned towards him as she sat down and brushed her lips against his cheek. It was the first time she had kissed him in public and he found the experience pleasing. He was even more pleased when she snuggled up close and hooked her arm through his, and when he realized that Mark's smile had become a trifle strained, he suddenly began to feel much better.

Success was relative and tonight he was the success, for he was the one with the pretty girl on his arm and Mark was alone and all the big hellos and the back-slapping had signified nothing.

'Where's your girl-friend tonight?' he said.

Mark shuffled uneasily in his chair. 'She's gone out with her husband.'

'Oh, I see.'

A lot of studied business across the table with cigarettes and matches and then Mark said: 'Coughlin didn't say anything about her, did he?'

'Coughlin? No. Why?'

Mark laughed, a short, not very confident sound. 'Well, he saw her, you see, when she came to pick me up at lunch that day. I didn't introduce them, of course. I thought it better not to. But I . . . I just wondered whether he'd said anything.'

'No,' Henry said. 'He didn't.' He was mystified by all this. That Mark, that shining light of the contemporary, meaningful society, should be embarrassed about going around with a married woman seemed quite out of character. And he was embarrassed, that was clear. It was all of three minutes since he had last snapped his fingers.

'It's all rather awkward,' he said. 'I keep asking her to come and live with me, permanently, but she can't seem to make up her mind. I think she's waiting to see how successful I am with the TV show before she decides. Well, you can't blame her, can you?' He addressed the question, appealingly, to the Jungle Bunny.

She hesitated. 'No,' she said. She said it as if she had been about to say something else but had changed her mind. But Mark took the answer at its face value and appeared grateful for it.

'That's what I think,' he said.

A waitress appeared beside them, leaning across to put a bill in front of Henry. There were sweat stains under her arms and down the middle of her tight trouser seat. She looked tired and old and she smelled stale.

'Beethoven would like you to go and have a drink with him and his friends,' she said to Mark.

He brightened at once. 'Hey, well . . .' He stopped and looked at the Jungle Bunny. 'Would you mind?'

'Not at all.' She smiled, shaking her head. 'We must be going anyway.'

'In that case . . . Tell him thanks and I'll be right over.' The waitress nodded wearily and went away.

'Well, I'll be seeing you around,' said Mark. He started to get up and then noticed the bill on the table. Before Henry could move he had picked it up and was bearing it off.

'Have this on me,' he said. 'Be good, kids.' He swaggered across the room, snapping his fingers and humming the refrain from 'I'm comin', baby, I'm comin'. The old Mark, on his way back where he belonged, among the famous.

'Are you coming home with me?' the Jungle Bunny asked.

Henry hadn't thought about it. Indeed, he had given no consideration at all to where he was going to sleep that night, except that he knew he could not face the prospect of going home. There had been vague ideas about booking in to a hotel but he had very little money on him and besides he didn't really want to be alone. He thought too much when he was alone.

'Yes,' he said. 'Please.' It couldn't make much difference now, anyway. Sue had already hanged him for a lamb. It would hardly make things worse if he went the whole way and became a sheep.

The Jungle Bunny gathered up her things and he steered her out with a farewell wave to Mark, who was wallowing contentedly in the company of a trio of pop-singers and their scrubbers.

'You don't like him much, do you?' the Jungle Bunny said when they came up into the Kings Road.

'No, not much.'

'He likes you, though.'

Henry was surprised. 'What makes you think so?'

'He wouldn't try so hard to impress you if he didn't.'

They walked in silence to the car and then Henry said: 'Do you like him?'

She shrugged. 'I feel sorry for him. The poor thing cnly really knows he exists when people are slapping him on the back.'

17. SUICIDE!

The same plate with the same egg congealing on it stood beside the sink and last night's discarded eyelashes were still crawling along the window-sill. They didn't seem to have got very far but then they probably weren't in much of a hurry.

'Coffee?' said the Jungle Bunny.

'Thanks.'

She made it quickly and sloppily. Nescafe and hot water, a dash of cold milk and too much sugar. They took their cups into the bed-sitter and sat down primly on opposite sides of the room.

'Have you left your wife then?' she asked.

'No. The other way round. She's walked out on me.'

'Oh dear. Are you sad about that?'

Henry shrugged.

'What are you going to do?'

'I'm damned if I know.'

She fell silent, gazing thoughtfully into the muddy depths of her cup. She did not ask him if he still loved Sue and he was glad about that. It was not a question he particularly wanted to face at that moment. To be in love with a wife who had left you seemed to Henry to be the very depths of humiliation and to admit such a thing, certainly to other people and possibly even to himself, would be to become a figure of fun.

'It's all because of me, isn't it?' said the Jungle Bunny.

'Well . . .' He hesitated. 'There were other things, too, but, yes, I suppose that was the clincher, all right.'

'I'm sorry.' She sounded as if she meant it, too.

'It's not your fault.'

She took the empty cups back to the kitchen and stacked them alongside the rest of the débris on the draining board. It never seemed to occur to her to wash up.

When she came back she said: 'Are you planning to shack up with me, then?'

'I don't know. Do you want me to?' He was sitting stiffly on an upright chair, hands resting on knees in a rather formal pose, as if he was being interviewed for a job.

'Permanently?' she said. 'I don't know. You don't love me, do you?'

'No,' said Henry. 'I don't.'

'I don't love you either.'

He didn't mind. It seemed a fair arrangement.

'I suppose we might grow to love each other,' she said doubtfully.

'Stranger things have happened,' he said, with an equal lack of conviction.

She wandered vaguely around the room, patting cushions and moving bits of clothing. It was not so much a matter of clearing up as of re-arranging the mess.

'It's late,' she said. 'We might as well go to bed.'

'Yes. Why not?'

She stripped off quickly and got into the bed and he undressed, too, with no self-consciousness this time. It was just as if he were at home. There was no excitement in undressing before Sue any more, nor in seeing her trim, long-legged body moving briskly and naked about the bedroom as she picked up odd bits of clothing. Excitement never lasted. What was a thrill the first time was habit the second and things were no different here. Already he and the Jungle Bunny were preparing for bed with as little embarrassment as if they had lived together for years. There must, he thought, be a moral in all that somewhere.

The sheets had not been changed. They were still grubby and crumpled and smelling of sin but he did not object to them any more. This, as it were, was the bed he had made and in which he must lie. This was how low-income adulterers lived, in second-hand flats with second-hand girls. Clean sheets and spotless bedrooms and neat little houses were the perks of the faithful, the just rewards of security and married bliss.

'How on earth did it all happen?' he wondered aloud, as he got in beside her. 'This, I mean – you and me and bed.'

'You fancied me, didn't you?' she rolled onto one side and put her hand on his stomach. Instinctively he tightened his muscles to disguise the little roll of fat around his middle.

'Yes, but I've fancied girls before and it's never led to this.'

'Ah, but the difference this time was that I fancied you, too, and I made up my mind to have you.'

She moved again and lay on top of him, her elbows on the pillow beside his head, her stomach against his stomach, her legs resting on top of his. She was a great deal heavier than he had expected and he found the position rather uncomfortable.

'What?' he said, breathlessly.

'I told you – remember? I'm the bird that pulls the fellers.'

'Oh, yes, so you did.' He had not really taken it all in the previous night and the enormity of her confession only now dawned upon him fully. 'Didn't you mind that I was married? Didn't it matter?'

Really, he thought piously, girls were becoming impossible these days. Cats would be ashamed to have morals like theirs. Here she was, slowly crushing the breath out of him and admitting, as though it were a perfectly natural thing – which to her it very probably was – that she had set out, quite coolly, to seduce a married man.

'If it didn't matter to you,' she said, 'it didn't matter to me.'

Good God, now she was throwing the blame back on him.

'That's not fair. It makes it sound as if I was on the lookout for a bit on the side.'

'Weren't you?'

Yes, perhaps he had been. In any event, he could not actually deny it. The fact that she had offered temptation was her business; the fact that he had accepted it was his. But even so it wasn't quite the way she made it sound. If he had been on the look-out for a small, extra-marital adventure it was not from lust or promiscuity but from defiance, because Sue had gone away from him a long time before she moved out of their house.

'Maybe,' he said.

'Are you comfortable?'

'No, not very.'

'I am,' she said. She stayed where she was. 'Tell me about your wife – she's a writer, isn't she? Is she successful?'

'It looks as if she will be.'

'That's nice.'

'Yes.'

'Are you a writer, too?'

'No,' he said, savagely. 'I'm a journalist. I'm a hack.'

She drew her head back and gave him a long, thoughtful look. 'Oh,' she said. 'I see.'

'What does that mean?' he asked, nastily.

'Quite a lot as a matter of fact. Now then, you've got a son, haven't you? Timothy, is it?'

'Look,' he said, 'do we have to talk about my family?' It didn't seem proper, somehow, considering the curious position they were in.

'Well, I'm not mad about it.' She groped experimentally with one hand. 'But you're not showing a lot of enthusiasm for anything else, are you?'

'Well, I'm not really in the mood for it tonight.'

'Oh, aren't you?' she said. 'We'll have to see about that.'

She lowered her whole weight onto his body, put her tongue in his mouth and with one hand she stroked his head while, with the other, she began to see about that.

Daylight forced its way between the heavy, faded curtains and revealed the shabbiness of the room more cruelly than artificial light could ever do. There was a large hole in the mock-Indian carpet, just by the door, and an enormous stain, coffee probably, beside the armchair.

The chair itself was leather and old with a bulgy, explosive look. All it seemed to need was one sudden assault by a heavily descending backside and springs would burst out in all directions like demons from a padded cell.

On the chest of drawers beneath the partly open window there was a thin layer of gritty dust thrown in by the traffic passing outside.

It was an extremely nasty room.

Henry shuddered and closed his eyes. He had seen enough and too much. The sheets looked even greyer and smelled even more sour this morning. They smelled of him and her and sleep and sex. They smelled of decay and ruin; his decay and ruin.

He was an inexperienced adulterer still and post-coital remorse – an emotion more wracking even than alcoholic remorse – had him in thrall.

Henry Tyson. Mr Nothing from Nowhere, and Nowhere was where he had got to. Forty-eight hours ago he was a securely if not particularly happily married man. Even twenty-four hours ago he still had a home and a family and now look at him. Oh, how were the lowly fallen . . .

Behind the closed lids, his eyes were hot and damp with tears. Timmy, he thought, oh, Timmy, Timmy, my son. Poor Timmy, what a mess your father is, what a walking, talking, fornicating mess.

Poor Timmy. Poor Sue. You deserved better than this, my darlings.

The tears oozed out between his lashes, and trickling slowly down the sides of his cheeks, came to rest in his ears.

Lord, he was getting maudlin again. What kind of a man, he demanded, are you? Why don't you do something? All right, but what – cut my throat?

If only he had brought his razor. It was typical. In all the crises of his life he never had the right equipment with him. Here, surely, would be the perfect place to end it all, here in this rotten bed in this rotten room. There would be a kind of aptness, almost a kind of justice, about terminating a life like his in a place like this.

He opened his eyes and saw the bottle of aspirin on the chest of drawers. A large bottle, unopened.

He got out of bed stealthily and pulled on his underpants. The Jungle Bunny stirred but slept on, her face smooth and young and pretty.

With the bottle in his hand he crept into the kitchen, filled a glass with water and, quietly, went through the bedroom to the door and out into the passage. The lavatory was at the far end, a small, stinking room with an archaic cistern from which small pieces of rust drifted down like dandruff.

He locked the door and opened the bottle . . .

Sue would be sorry when his body was discovered, when she realized the fearful end to which life and her lack of forgiveness had driven him. He imagined his body stretched out on the floor, the limbs gracefully arranged, his left, best, profile uppermost, the fingers of one hand still curling lightly round the empty aspirin bottle.

But no, it wouldn't work. A legless midget couldn't lie stretched out in this room.

The mental picture changed. He imagined his body . . . where? All squashed up between the lavatory pan and the wall, probably;

head down and backside jutting grotesquely into the air. Yes, that was more his style.

With a weary sigh he set about committing suicide . . .

After six aspirins he changed his mind. By then he had drunk all the water and he was feeling sick. Besides, the sheer mathematics of the task were beginning to depress him.

From the bed to the kitchen to fill the glass and from there across the bedroom, down the passage and into the lavatory had taken, say, one minute. Drinking the water and swallowing the aspirins had taken perhaps two minutes. Three minutes in all.

A second journey to the kitchen and back to refill the glass would take probably two minutes. Plus a further two minutes to get rid of six more aspirins.

There were 200 aspirins in the bottle and assuming that these were enough to kill him and working it out at his present rate of half a pint of water to six tablets he would have to make at least thirty-two more trips to the kitchen and drink about seventeen pints of water, taking a total time of two hours and eleven minutes before the bottle was empty.

It was impossible. In the first place he was pretty sure he couldn't drink all that water without drowning and in the second place if he was going to be trudging back and forth along the passage for the next two hours it was a pretty fair bet that somebody, the Jungle Bunny most likely, would find out what he was up to and stop him. He might just as well abandon the whole idea now.

He raised the lavatory seat, stuck two fingers down his throat and vomited gloomily into the bowl. When he had done that he leaned against the wall, thinking over the events of the past ten minutes and after a little while he began to giggle.

'Well,' the Jungle Bunny said, 'we still haven't decided, you know. What are we going to do?'

They were in a café at Earl's Court, drinking milky coffee out of glass cups and eating croissants. She looked extremely pretty in something denim and pink and she kept dunking her roll into the cup and sucking the soggy end with the uninhibited enthusiasm of a child. Henry wished she wouldn't do that. It made him feel quite sick again.

Actually, there were a number of things about her that were beginning to irritate him. The flare of her nostrils when she inhaled deeply on a cigarette. The way she left her hairpins on the breadboard at the flat. The untidiness with which she distributed left-off clothing all over the place, so that it was impossible to sit anywhere without first removing a crumpled sweater or a brassiere that peered up from the seat of the chair like a pair of huge, bulging eyes.

All these things depressed and alarmed him largely because he was so aware of them. They were beginning to make an impression upon him in the way that other people's habits only do when you know you are going to have to live with them.

Was he really that committed? Was this to be his life from now on – shacked up with the Jungle Bunny in a series of drab flats?

She, at least, seemed to assume so, for she said again: 'Well, what, then?'

He shrugged helplessly. 'I dunno.'

'That's not much good, is it? You *must* know. Are you going to move in with me or aren't you?'

'Do you want me to?'

'I don't care. It's up to you. I mean, it's really all over with your wife, is it?'

'Looks like it.'

'Well, then.'

Well, then, what? He had to stay somewhere and until he had sorted his finances out, somewhere cheap. Precisely where he came to rest hardly seemed to matter. None of it seemed real, anyway. Deep down he was unable to convince himself that it was truly all over, that on the strength of one bunk-up, Sue had moved out and left him for ever. It was absurd. Wasn't it?

'I'd better call S . . . my wife,' he said, 'and fix up the arrangements.'

'What arrangements?' The Jungle Bunny thrust another roll into her cup and sucked it noisily. A layer of grease and breadcrumbs floated on the surface of her coffee. Henry turned his eyes away. Could he live with a sight like that every morning of his life?

'I don't know,' he said, vaguely. 'There must be some arrangements you have to make when a marriage breaks up. You know, money and the house and . . . and our little boy.'

'All right.' She didn't appear to be greatly interested in Henry's arrangements. 'So you'll move in with me?'

'Yes. If that's all right.'

'Sure. You'll chip in for rent and food and that?'

'Of course.' This was all wrong. It was too undramatic, too matter-of-fact. The trouble with the Permissive Society, he reflected sadly, was that it had killed romance.

'I'll see you tonight then, shall I?' she asked.

'Yes, I suppose so.' He realized suddenly that he had no idea what she did all day long. Until now she had simply been someone who appeared at night and took him into her bed. He seemed to recall that she had said she was a dancer but surely that wasn't a day-time occupation.

'What are your plans?' he asked. 'For today, I mean.'

'I've got a little modelling job at eleven and this afternoon I'm going to an audition for the chorus of a new musical.'

'Oh. Well . . . good luck.'

She shook her head. 'I don't think I've got a chance. They want white girls, really.'

It came as a shock. In a curious way, except for the moment when Morgan pointed her out in the street and the first time he slept with her he had never been strongly conscious of her colour.

'Is that much of a handicap?' he said. 'You know, being . . . well, not Caucasian?'

She held her coffee cup in both hands and surveyed him broodingly over the rim. 'A handicap? Being a wog? Well, yes, you might just say it does sometimes make things the teeniest, weeniest bit difficult.'

He flushed. 'Sorry. Silly question. Only I'd never thought of you as . . . well, as . . .'

'A wog? Go on, say it. Wog. Or spade, if you like. It's quite easy. Wog. Or spade. Like that.'

'Well, I hadn't,' he said, stubbornly.

'That's nice of you, Henry. I don't think it's really true but it's nice of you anyway.'

They finished their breakfasts in silence. Then Henry said: 'Where do your parents live?'

'Liverpool.' She pushed her plate to one side and briskly swept the breadcrumbs from the plastic tablecloth in front of her onto the floor. 'Dad's a doctor. He's only got wog patients, of course, except for a handful of poor whites but he seems happy enough. Well, I suppose it's better than driving a bus.'

'You're a funny girl.' He felt a renewed onsurge of tenderness for her.

'Am I? Perhaps I am. I don't know.' She lit a cigarette with the studied, rather brittle nonchalance she had assumed as soon as she started talking about herself.

'Family?' Henry asked.

'Two brothers and a sister, all at school.' She looked up at the clock above the counter. 'I must go,' she said.

When they got outside she kissed him quickly on the cheek and ducked away into the traffic. 'See you tonight,' she called back over her shoulder. 'Ring me if you're going to be late.'

Henry watched her go, hips swinging, pink skirt bouncing against her thighs. He felt depressed again. Already, he thought, she was behaving like a wife. One quick passionless peck on the cheek, a brief instruction which he would ignore at his peril and she was gone. It didn't seem at all the way a mistress should take leave of her lover.

He stopped at a barber's for a shave and then went to the office. Except that he approached it from a different direction and from the bed of a different woman he was just as he was every other morning – a domestic animal about to earn the wherewithal to keep the nest going.

15. MORE TROUBLE WITH COUGHLIN

Coughlin wanted him. Henry was not surprised. His professional day always seemed to start with Coughlin wanting him.

'He seemed very impatient,' Bilbow said. 'Perhaps he's really going to fire you this time.'

Henry shrugged. 'Could be.' He didn't care. One way and another he had so many problems already that a small thing like being fired would hardly be noticeable among them.

He phoned Surbiton but there was no reply. Sue's parents would be at work by this time but where could she and Timmy be? Shopping, perhaps, or . . . On an off-chance he phoned his home but there was no answer there, either. He was relieved in a way because he was not at all sure what he would say to Sue if he did contact her. Of course, he would have to think about that sometime but not yet. Thinking about Sue – really thinking about her – was turning out to be a painful process and he didn't want to do too much of it until the wounds healed a bit.

'Coughlin,' Bilbow said, 'is waiting for you.'

'I wonder what he wants.'

'No idea.' Bilbow took off his glasses and began to polish them, squinting blindly with his large milky eyes in Henry's direction. 'Sure to be something meaningful, though.'

Henry shook his head. 'No, that's changed. Everything's contemporary now.'

'Is it? I'll make a note of that.'

'Yes,' Henry said, 'you'd better. You don't want to be caught wearing last month's word.'

To his mild astonishment he found Coughlin in his office. Mark Payne was there, too.

It was a nice office, bright and modern. Henry wondered why Coughlin did not conduct more of his conferences there, rather than in the executive lavatory. Perhaps it was because almost anyone could have an office but not everyone had a key to the executive lavatory. Coughlin did and there was no point in possessing a status symbol of such magnitude unless you flourished it.

'You're late,' Coughlin said. It was five past ten and Henry was working the 10 till 6 shift that day. He had in fact, already been in the building for seven minutes. 'I won't have my reporters sloping in and out whenever they feel like it. I want them in on time, understand?'

'But . . .' Henry protested.

'Sit down,' Coughlin said. With the true instinct of the bully he knew the advantage of suspending hostilities before the victim had a chance to fight back.

There were only two comfortable chairs in the room and Coughlin and Mark were in possession of them. Henry sat on a fragile, tubular affair with a hard, black, plastic seat. He nodded a greeting to Mark and got another nod back.

'All right,' Coughlin said. 'Now I think we're all agreed, aren't we, that the age of the Permissive Society is coming to an end?'

He made this statement with great confidence as, indeed, he made all his statements, whether the evidence supported him or not. In this case Henry was not at all sure that the evidence did support him. As far as he could recall his route to the office that very morning had taken him past numerous bookshops and cinemas whose wares seemed to proclaim that permissiveness, in the sense of total sexual abandonment, was not simply a way of life but the only possible way of life.

'Well . . .' he said.

'Exactly.' Coughlin nodded. 'So, the question is: what do we do about it?'

He sat back, sharp and eager in his trendy executive suit, and silence filled the room. Henry stared at Mark and Mark stared back. Their expressions were identically bemused. What were they *expected* to do about it? Coughlin might have given a clue.

'Well?' Coughlin demanded.

Henry said, hesitantly: 'What I'm not entirely sure about is, are we glad or are we sorry? I mean, are we going to run a campaign to put trousers on dogs or do we want sex on the National Health?'

'What?' Coughlin said, blankly. 'Don't be a bloody fool. No, what I mean is: how are we going to record the end of the permissive era?'

'Precisely,' Mark said as if he had understood that point all along. He gave a sincere sniff and joined Coughlin in a glance of reproach at Henry.

'What we need,' Coughlin said, musingly, 'is a meaningful, contemporary piece of compulsive sociological reporting.' Four months' words in one sentence – it was an all-comers record. Henry was so excited he almost applauded. 'That's where you come in, Mark.'

'Is it? Ah.' Mark stared thoughtfully at the grey carpet. He didn't seem very pleased.

'Of course, it'll need some pretty exhaustive research. You agree, Tyson?'

'I suppose so,' Henry said. He was still trying to fathom out what Coughlin was getting at.

'What do you mean, you suppose so? I *say* so.'

'It'll need some pretty exhaustive research,' Henry said.

'Exactly. Now my theory is that the mini-skirt is almost entirely responsible for all the promiscuity we see around us.' He paused, awaiting the effect of this philosophical bombshell.

Henry said: 'A lot of that about, is there?'

'What?'

'Promiscuity. Lot of it about, you think?'

'Of course there is,' Coughlin snapped, irritably. 'It's one of the rottenest fruits of the Permissive Society. Good phrase, that. You might bear it in mind, Mark.'

'What?' Mark looked up. 'Oh. Yes, I will. Greg, this research...'

Coughlin held up a hand. 'I'm coming to that. First, though, I'd like to outline my ideas.' He propped his feet on the desk and frowned reflectively at the ceiling. 'What we want to do is to attack the Permissive Society through the mini-skirt, in other words to trace it all the way back to the time when women first started flaunting their legs and their buttocks in open invitation. You remember those days – before tights? Everywhere you looked there was nothing but suspenders and thighs?'

'Yes,' Henry said. 'Good old days, they were.'

Coughlin ignored him. He had a fervent, visionary look in his eye. 'The Permissive Society has gone far enough – too far. The time has come to cry halt. That's our line. You agree, Mark?'

'Yes. Splendid. Greg, about this research . . .'

'Quite, quite. Now then . . .'

'Excuse me,' Henry said, politely, 'but I don't think I quite understand.' He scratched his head in genuine puzzlement, for though he was well used to the fact that newspaper executives changed their minds and attitudes with no more thought than they would devote to changing their socks, Coughlin's present volte-face was a little too dramatic to be taken all at once. Had he not, just a few days ago, put forward the idea that Mark Payne should write a piece in *praise* of the Permissive Society, or at least in praise of permissive and liberal people? 'I always thought you were in favour of the Permissive Society.'

'Me?' Coughlin said. He laughed indulgently. 'Good Lord, no. I've always been most strongly opposed to it.'

Henry grinned, a weak sort of grin clearly destined to die an early death. 'But only the other day you said . . .'

'You must have misunderstood me,' Coughlin said, not at all indulgently. Good Heavens, was a man to have something he said as long ago as Tuesday held against him now? 'As a matter of fact, I was discussing the matter only last night with the chairman. Strange coincidence, really. It turned out we were in complete agreement about the disastrous effect the Permissive Society and, of course, the mini-skirt have had on public morals. Actually, the chairman felt even more strongly about the mini-skirt than I did. Kept returning to the subject. You could see he'd given it a lot of thought. Amazingly aware of its effect, he was, for a man of his age . . .'

Light dawned. 'Ah,' Henry said. 'Of course. Forgive me.'

Coughlin surveyed him narrowly but Henry's expression was blandly innocent. And indeed he could see all now. The chairman was opposed to the Permissive Society (probably because he was no longer getting his share and was living bitterly on the memory of all those thighs he used to see about when the mini was in fashion); therefore the *Daily Journal* was opposed to the Permissive Society; therefore Coughlin was opposed to the Permissive Society. It was all perfectly straightforward once you understood the one basic, all-important fact.

Yet it was nonetheless alarming. Was the Permissive Society to die for no better reason than that the chairman and Coughlin said so? Had Henry, its newest member, once again joined too late? Was he to be left alone, shamefully practising permissiveness in shady places, while the rest of the country returned to a life of abstinence and self-discipline? He found it hard to avoid the gloomy conclusion that he had made the most awful mess of things just lately.

'Well, Mark,' Coughlin said. 'What do you think?'

Mark took off his glasses and frowned with slightly myopic sincerity as he wiped them. 'Sounds good,' he said, at length. 'The only thing is, will it clash with my image? After all, I'm supposed to be one of the leaders of the liberated people, their spokesman if you like. I don't want to knock my own position.' Snap, snap.

Coughlin put a hand on Mark's shoulder to show that when it came to sincerity he was up there with the front runners. 'Mark, if we handle this properly you'll be *the* leader of the liberated people. It's not a reactionary step we're taking, you know. It's a bold leap forward – the knocking down of an old trend and the establishment of a new one. Permissiveness is a shackle, that's the point I want to put across. It's a stranglehold on people's lives. It's a . . . it's a blinker that narrows their vision and restricts their awareness of the richness life has to offer when sex is put in its proper, secondary place. God, I wish we had a secretary here to take notes, with all these ideas flying about.'

Mark thought about Coughlin's credo. He also thought about the money Coughlin was paying him. He put his glasses back on. 'Right,' he said.

'Tyson? What are your thoughts?'

'Eh? Ah. Yes.' Henry really had no thoughts, although it did occur to him to wonder what he was supposed to be doing there in the first place. 'Well . . .' he said. A thought came to him. 'Yes, one thing bothers me a bit. Could you explain just what the mini-skirt has to do with all the promiscuity that's apparently going on now? I mean, nobody wears mini-skirts any more.'

Coughlin thumped the desk in exasperation. 'Have you been listening?' he said. 'Have you been listening *at all*? What we're embarking on here is a series, a *major* series – not just a one-off thinkpiece. Look, let me spell it out: we're looking into all our country's ills – the promiscuity, the idleness, the disaffection, the strikes, the cynicism, the political unrest. And what's the underlying cause of all that? Eh? Can you tell me?'

Henry thought about it. 'Harold Macmillan telling us we'd never had it so good?' he suggested.

'God give me strength!' Coughlin said, thumping his forehead in disbelief. 'What do you know about bloody Harold Macmillan? Look, I'm telling you what the underlying cause is. It's the Permissive Society, right? The idea that everyone can do what he wants and get what he wants and never have to work for it. So what we are going to do is to trace the Permissive Society right back to the beginning and in the beginning was the mini-skirt. Right?'

Henry did his best to absorb all this and then he nodded and said: 'Why? I mean, why the mini-skirt? How did the mini-skirt start all this trouble?'

Coughlin gave him another narrow, suspicious look. He suspected almost everybody at one time or another of trying to send him up but Henry most of all.

'I should have thought it was perfectly obvious,' he said, sharply. 'It made it easier to get there.'

'Where?' Henry said.

Coughlin turned away in slight embarrassment. 'You know,' he said. 'There.'

'Oh, I see. Yes. There.'

'Precisely.' Coughlin looked relieved. He had a mild puritanica streak and he never liked to be specific about the more intimate parts of the human body if he could avoid it. 'And that was the start of all our troubles. Easy sex and the overthrowing of all accepted standards. Now, to give our series its historical sweep, its socio-historical sweep if you like, we must look again at the mini-skirt and what it signified. That's the main thing, you see: the mini-skirt is a symbol, it was the warning sign which we ignored . . .'

'I don't agree with you,' Henry said.

'What?'

'I don't agree. That the mini-skirt meant easy sex. What do you think, Mark?'

'Well,' Mark said, carefully.

'But it's obvious. Good God, I should have thought any fool could see that. If a girl's wearing a mini-skirt you only have to stick your hand three inches up it and you've got your finger on the button. You're there. And if you touch a girl there . . .'

'You have to marry her?' Henry said, helpfully.

'No! You're practically in bed with her, that's what I mean. Dammit, you don't even have to take her skirt off – just hitch it up and the target area's completely exposed. Am I right?'

Henry became deeply aware of his left shirt cuff. It was grubby. So was the right one and he remembered that he had brought no change of clothing when he left home. He ought to do something about that.

'Of course you're right, Greg,' Mark said. 'Certainly.'

'Exactly. But on the other hand when girls wore skirts down below their knees and you stuck a hand up, what happened? You grabbed a fistful of knee. Well, I don't have to tell you that the difference between grabbing a girl's knee and her . . . her . . . groin is, well, the difference between chalk and cheese.'

Chalk and cheese, Henry thought. Yes.

'Besides,' Coughlin went on, 'before you could get past the knee the girl would have got up and walked away. And if she was wearing a tight skirt you'd *never* get past the knee without breaking your arm.'

He stopped and glanced intently from Henry to Mark. 'It all seems self-evident to me,' he said.

Henry watched him, wondering how far he ought to go. Coughlin could be dangerous when opposed but on the other hand he really couldn't be allowed to get away with all this nonsense.

'I still don't agree,' Henry said.

Anger and Coughlin never seemed to be far apart when Henry was around and now they had a dramatic reunion. 'God Almighty!' he said.

Recklessly now, Henry said: 'Look, either a girl will let you stick your hand up her skirt or she won't. If she will, you're laughing, if she won't, you aren't and it doesn't matter whether her skirt covers her ankles or is up round her neck.'

Coughlin took a deep breath. His face grew redder and his eyes protruded. 'You've missed the point!' he cried.

'What?' Henry said.

'You've missed the bloody point!'

The door opened quietly and Jennifer Clovis came in bearing copy in her hand. She opened her mouth to say something, closed it again when she realized a row was in progress and tiptoed softly over to stand beside Coughlin's chair. She was wearing a pale blue mini-skirt.

Coughlin said, furiously: 'Look, I'm not talking about whether girls let you put your hand up or whether they don't. All I'm talking about is how easy it is to do it. Don't you understand?'

'Well, no, I . . .'

'Christ!' Coughlin sat up straight, waving his hands wildly in his frustration. 'If a girl's wearing a long skirt you *can't* get your hand up it. If she's wearing a mini-skirt it's the easiest thing in the world. It's . . . You . . . Good God, all you have to do is this!'

Whereupon to the intense surprise of his entire audience his right hand shot out and disappeared up Clovis's skirt. The girl gave a squeak of alarm, clapped her legs together and took a swift jump backwards and Coughlin, his hand firmly trapped between her strong, round thighs, went with her, toppling sideways out of his chair and scrabbling frantically at his desk with his free hand for support.

While this was in progress the door opened again and the editor looked in. 'Oh . . . er . . . Greg,' he said, 'I . . .' The full significance of the tableau that presented itself to him dawned suddenly and he recoiled. 'Good *God*!' he said and went out again.

For a moment everyone in the room remained still. Then Clovis opened her legs, warily, and Coughlin's hand fell out of her skirt like a dead bird from its nest.

He straightened up and looked around him.

'Ha, ha,' he said.

Nobody else laughed and after that first effort Coughlin didn't bother either. An air of embarrassment had settled upon the room.

Clovis said: 'I think I'd better come back later.'

'Yes. Yes, do that,' Coughlin bestowed a weak smile upon her. 'I'm . . . er . . . sorry about all this. I'll explain when you come back.'

'Yes.' She went out, still blushing.

'Well,' Coughlin said. He cleared his throat. 'Rather awkward that. I hope the editor didn't . . . er . . . didn't think that . . . er . . .'

'I shouldn't worry,' Henry said. 'Probably thought you were just having a bit of a grope. *Droits de seigneur* or something.'

Coughlin turned upon him quite savagely as if under the impression that Henry was responsible for the entire unhappy incident. 'I think we've wasted enough time!' he snarled. 'Let's get on with it. You know the kind of series I want. Are there any questions?'

Mark said: 'Well, there is one thing, Greg. This research you were talking about. I'm not quite sure what kind of research you had in mind but I don't think I'll have time for it anyway. I'm terribly busy with the programme and . . .'

Coughlin looked easier now. They were back on the kind of ground he understood well, the discussion of technicalities, details, and as if to brush aside all memories of his recent embarrassment he interrupted briskly.

'I'd thought of that,' he said. 'Of course, we can't expect you to do that sort of work. That's why Tyson's here – he'll do the research.'

He paused and glanced at Henry. So did Mark.

'Couldn't have chosen a better man,' Mark said. Snap, snap. He had his sincere face on. Coughlin nodded. He was looking at Henry like a general at a subaltern to whom he had just given an order which would, of course, be obeyed instantly and without question.

'No,' Henry said.

Coughlin and Mark stopped looking at Henry and looked at each other instead, the former thunderstruck, the latter frowning sincerely.

'I beg your pardon,' Coughlin said.

'No,' Henry said. 'I'm not paid to do leg-work.' He was amazed at his own temerity but determined, too. Whatever fate might have in store for him he was quite certain that running errands for Mark Payne would be no part of it.

'You are paid,' Coughlin said, 'to do whatever I tell you to do. And if I tell you to research for an important sociological series then . . .'

'Important!' Henry said, furiously. 'It's a load of rubbish. Good Lord, am I the only sane man left? Can't you see what utter crap it is? We've been sitting here, three more or less intelligent men, for half an hour discussing this ludicrous project as if it meant something and now you're asking me to do research on it so this idiot can write it. What kind of research? Eh? Have you any idea?'

'Tyson,' Coughlin said, bulging and red again. 'Don't push it, Tyson. I warn you . . .'

'What am I supposed to do?' Henry asked, sweeping this warning recklessly aside. 'Stop women in the streets and ask them whether wearing mini-skirts had ever made them promiscuous? Or do you want practical demonstrations like the one you just gave us? Shall I creep up on girls in the Tube and stick my rigid index finger up their . . .'

'Tyson,' Coughlin said, sharply enough to cut him short. His eyes still bulged but he had turned white instead of red and his voice had gone very quiet. 'You're refusing an assignment, a bona fide assignment. All right. There's no more to be said. You may go.'

Henry stood up. He had not expected it to end quite as swiftly as this and he was feeling uncertain and extremely apprehensive. A roaring, ranting Coughlin he could understand and, to an extent, cope with. This quiet, menacing Coughlin was altogether more frightening. His own anger ebbed fast to be replaced by a dour sullenness. He glanced at Mark but Mark was staring at the carpet with sincere intensity and snapping his fingers to show how much excess energy was bubbling up inside him.

Henry went slowly to the door and when he reached it, Coughlin said softly: 'Tyson. Do you want to change your mind?'

Henry looked back. To hell with it – why not? All right, he'd lose face but he'd save his job. His position vis-à-vis Mark Payne would be clearly established for ever as one of definite inferiority but did that matter? He would be a legman but so what? He would have surrendered finally to Coughlin and all the other Coughlins of the newspaper industry but what difference would that make? Coughlin was offering him another chance, probably his last chance. So what the hell – why not take it?

He drew a deep breath. 'No,' he said. 'No, I don't.'

Coughlin nodded, slowly. 'Then I'll crucify you,' he said.

19. MORGAN'S TALE

There was a woman standing beside the bar, a young, slim woman with an attractive figure and when she turned to greet a newly arrived friend it became perfectly clear that she was not wearing a bra. Her breasts, small and firm and plainly outlined against the material of her blouse, were pleasing to the eye and it occurred to Henry that only a few years ago the sight of those untrammelled nipples staring at him with vast disdain across the room would have shocked him as much as they excited him.

Now they had neither effect. They had no effect at all. Well, that wasn't quite true. He may not have been excited or shocked but he was certainly interested and that was what the girl wanted. Wasn't it? For the past ten years and more women had been going around in the kind of brazen, skimpy clothes that even the hookers on the beat would not have dared to wear when he was younger, so obviously they wanted men to look, to show their appreciation and their interest. He looked at the girl again and smiled to show his appreciation and his interest but she didn't smile back. The cool blue eyes and the hard brown nipples stared him down unblinkingly. For a moment he was disconcerted, wondering whether his smile could have converted itself, without his permission, into a leer. Surely not. He wasn't the leering type. Perhaps then the display wasn't intended for him but for somebody else. Or perhaps it wasn't even intended as a display at all. Perhaps the girl had left her bra at home because it was a warm, summer's day and on a figure such as hers a bra would be more of an encumbrance than an asset, since it could fulfil no useful purpose and would only serve to make her chest hot.

Coughlin was out of touch, he thought. All that itchy brooding over mini-skirts and thighs. The day of the legman had gone and the titman had come into his own. And yet even that was probably an over-simplification. What was happening, Henry suspected, was that women were slowly cooling the atmosphere, educating men by degrees to a point at which they could contemplate a female body without necessarily yelping like randy puppies. For several years women had allowed men to look at their legs and when legs had finally become an accepted part of the landscape, no more remarkable than trees or lamp posts, they had switched attention to their breasts. In a year or so breasts, too, would become as commonplace as poached eggs or water melons and then women would attract men's gaze to some other part of their anatomies, saying: 'All right, now you know about legs and you know about boobs, so get used to this,' until eventually woman as a species would cease to be a general object of sexual desire and men would start to concern themselves with such other qualities as she might possess. It was a long-term project, Henry thought, but he supposed it would work in the end; women's projects usually did.

Coughlin, therefore, was doubly wrong. He didn't understand women at all. He didn't even understand that though a short skirt or a breast-revealing blouse might provoke lust in the beholder it did not follow, by any means, that they also indicated promiscuity in the wearer. As subtle instruments in woman's Greater Plan these things were neither an invitation to bed nor even, necessarily, an incitement to day-dream . . .

'You're not listenin' to me, are you?' Morgan said. He was eating sausages and mash at the table beside Henry and his voice held the aggrieved note of one who had been imparting matters of great moment and had been totally ignored for his pains.

'I was thinking,' Henry said. Even before the girl's breasts had caught his attention he had been thinking, albeit of other things.

After leaving Coughlin's office he had gone up to Fleet Street for a coffee and the opportunity to reflect in comparative solitude on what he had just done. Marriage one day, job the next. He could imagine what they'd say in the Press Club – 'Not a man to do things by halves, old Tyson. Chucked away the lot, just like that. Anybody know what he's doing these days?'

When he returned to the office, two things were brought to his attention. The first was a notice pinned to the reporters' board and signed G. R. J. Coughlin.

'There has been a tendency in the paper recently,' it said, 'to glorify the so-called "Permissive Society" and to denigrate the so-called "Suburban Life." We must watch this closely. Never forget that the *Daily Journal* is essentially a family newspaper and that families tend to live in suburbs. Let us not start sneering at morality and the worthwhile human virtues while extolling the cheap and gimmicky people who lead flashy, amoral and immoral lives . . .'

There was a bit more in similar style but Henry didn't bother to read it. He felt sick enough already.

And the second thing that was brought to his attention was the fact that Coughlin wished to see him.

'After lunch.' the news editor had said, passing on the message. 'In his office – about three.'

There were no jokes that day and no hostility either. Both the news editor and his acolytes treated him with a remote coolness as if they did not wish to be involved with him in any way. Henry recognized the signals. He was on the way out and that was a contagious condition in a newspaper office. It was not safe even to spit upon people so afflicted for that meant getting close to them and to be seen in the proximity of a man on the way out was to plant suspicion in the minds of others that one might be sympathetic towards the afflicted. Very dangerous, that was.

Henry was given no work to do and the only show business story to break that morning was passed to someone else. Henry spent his time on the telephone trying to reach Sue but without success. After his tenth abortive call he decided she was avoiding him. Smart lad, that Tyson. Not slow on the uptake, you know.

Christ, what a mess . . .

Just before one, Morgan called. 'Hello, darlin'. You eating?'

'Might as well,' Henry said, dully.

'Right. Where – Granny's?'

'Yeah. Granny's.'

The pub was actually called The Chessboard but nobody ever referred to it as anything but Granny's, though the origin of this name was long since forgotten. Downstairs it was dark and Victorian with a long, ornate bar and tiled walls like a public lavatory and a lunch counter that served sandwiches and hot snacks. Upstairs it was contemporary and garish, all chrome and Formica and the food in the restaurant there was expensive but good.

Henry and Morgan sat downstairs, drank beer and ate sausages and – in at least one case – brooded.

'Well, if you don't bleedin' well want to listen I won't tell you then,' Morgan said, crossly.

'Sorry, sorry. I'm listening.' Henry pushed his plate away, drank some of his beer and lit a cigarette.

'I should have thought you'd have been interested,' Morgan said, managing to sound querulous even though his mouth was full of bread and potato.

'Yes, I am, I'm interested. Very. What were you saying?'

Satisfied now that he had his companion's full attention, Morgan took his time. He ate the last of his sausage, wiped his plate round with a chunk of bread, ate that, drank some beer and sighed.

'Ah, that's better. Not bad, was it?'

'No,' Henry said. 'Not bad. Now, what were you saying?'

'Well, of course, if you really don't want to know . . .'

'Sod it,' Henry said. Didn't he have enough on his mind, without Morgan going all coy and sensitive on him? 'Tell me if you want to, otherwise shut up.'

Morgan's small, sharp eyes, salesman's eyes, looked him over, craftily. 'I saw your missus last night,' he said.

'You what?' Henry sat up. A cliché, he thought, even as he did it. People in books were always doing that – 'He sat up.' Quite so. Give people a shock and that's what they did – they sat up. 'Where?'

'American bar, Savoy.' Morgan blew smoke out, his rather feminine mouth puckering into a soft pink bow. 'It was after that party we were at. You know? Well, I just dropped in to have one for the road and there she was . . .'

Morgan had taken the large TV starlet there and fed her Negronis while he felt her leg under the table and thought about the many happy hours he would spend bouncing about on top of her. After four Negronis he was just going to suggest that they moved on when the small TV producer came bustling up.

'Ah, there you are, darling.' He leaned down, not that he had to lean very far, and splosh, a fat, wet kiss spread itself all over the starlet's left cheek. At once she got up, reaching for gloves and hand bag,

and the producer grabbed her possessively by the arm.

'Goodbye, old boy,' he said to Morgan. 'Good of you to look after her for me . . . Come along, darling, we must hurry. The others are waiting.'

The starlet blew Morgan a kiss with lips like Michelin tyres and then the two of them were away, arm in arm, their hips bumping together as they hurried down to the foyer.

'Cow's son!' Morgan called after them, or more specifically after the producer, but they didn't seem to hear him. He sat moodily for a while, staring into his glass and then Sue murmured 'Hello, Morgan' and sat down beside him.

'Who was she with?' Henry asked, sharply. He was excited in a very unpleasant kind of way. It was trepidation, really, a conviction that he was about to hear something that was definitely not to his advantage. His nerve ends were quivering and he was breathing fast.

'Nobody,' Morgan said. 'She'd been with her agent or something but he'd gone off to a dinner date.'

Henry was silent. Then he said: 'I suppose she told you?'

'About how she'd walked out on you? Yeah.'

Morgan had asked her where Henry was and so she had indeed told him. 'I've left him,' she said.

'No!' Morgan's little eyes had shone. 'Why?'

She ran her hand through her straight, golden hair, a very feminine gesture that reminded Morgan of what a very feminine and very attractive woman she was. 'Oh, I don't know. A lot of reasons, I suppose. Things have been very odd lately. Henry hasn't been happy and I haven't been happy and . . . oh, then he went off with a woman.' She looked up pushing the tousled hair away from her eyes. 'I expect you knew about that.'

'Yeah,' Morgan said, nodding.

He accepted another pint of bitter from Henry and sucked at it noisily. 'Trying to pump me, she was,' he said. 'About who the bird was.'

'You didn't tell her, I hope?'

'No! Think I'm daft?'

No, Morgan hadn't told her Not old Morgan, although she'd tried hard enough to squeeze the information from him, both at the Savoy and later over dinner in a Soho trattoria.

'Morgan, why won't you tell me?' she had asked, plaintively. The grey eyes were huge and earnest and as she leaned forward her body moved sweetly beneath her summer dress.

'Wouldn't be fair, darlin', would it?'

'But I want to know. I've got to know, can't you see that? It's rotten not knowing who he's with and why and what she's got that I haven't. Morgan, you know her – what's she got that I haven't?'

Morgan inspected her carefully; a potential buyer looking over the livestock. 'I dunno. She's thinner than you for a start. Not much tit but a nice arse.'

'Oh.' Sue thought about this gravely. She had had quite a lot to drink. 'Well, what's wrong with my arse?'

'Nothing. I was clocking it as we came in. Very nice.'

Sue made a clucking sound with her tongue and her teeth and dropped a small bread pellet into her wine glass. She was leaning on her left elbow with her fingers entwined in her hair and she looked very young.

'Well, what does she look like – is she blonde or dark?'

'Dark,' Morgan said. 'Yes. Definitely dark. Very dark.'

'Oh.' Her voice was small and sad. 'He always used to like blondes. I suppose . . . I suppose after me he's gone off them. Morgan, tell me . . .'

Morgan stood up. 'Come on, darlin', I'll run you home.'

'Men!' she said angrily. 'It's always the same. You stick together like . . . like . . .'

'Shit to a blanket. I know. Come on.'

'So you never told her who the girl was?' Henry said. He was most anxious about that. It was better that Sue didn't know.

'I told you – 'course I didn't. I just gave her a lift home to her old woman's place and left her, didn't I?'

He had driven her back to Surbiton and stopped the car a few yards from her parents' house. Sue's head had cleared during the drive and when they pulled up she said: 'Thank you, Morgan, you've been terribly sweet.'

He took her wrist as she started to open the door. 'Don't go. Have a last fag.' He put a cigarette in her hand and had his lighter out and working before she could refuse.

'I suppose you're sort of at a loose end now, then?' he said. 'I mean, you haven't got a feller in mind or anything, have you?'

'No,' Sue shook her head. In the glow of her cigarette the grey eyes were watchful.

'I was thinking,' Morgan said. He shuffled his buttocks surreptitiously along the seat towards her. 'You know, maybe I could take you out sometime. I mean, seeing it's all over with you and Henry . . .'

'Yes?' There was something in her expression, something almost mocking. Morgan glanced away uneasily. The seat creaked softly as his buttocks edged a little closer.

'I fancy you,' he said.

'I expect you fancy a lot of girls.'

'Yes,' Morgan said contentedly. 'Yes, I do. But some I fancy more than others, know what I mean?' He reached for her thigh and she picked his hand up delicately with her thumb and forefinger and put it down on the seat between them.

'Do you sleep around a lot?' she asked.

'Yeah. Well, you know, a fair bit. Me and my wife don't get on all that well and so, well, I go off with the occasional bird.'

Sue nodded. 'No more than Henry though, I expect.' There seemed to be a note of perverse pride in her voice and Morgan, justifiably nettled at the implication that his manhood was being unfavourably compared with that of her husband, leapt in to put the record straight.

'Henry!' he said. 'Henry? You've got to be joking.'

'Oh,' Sue said, shaking her head inquiringly. 'Not much of a ram?'

'No. Not a ram at all.'

'I see.' She stared thoughtfully out at the darkness of the street and Morgan put his arm around her shoulder.

'Listen,' he said, 'do you have to go in now? Couldn't we . . .'

'No,' she kissed him lightly and briskly on the lips. 'We couldn't. But thanks for asking, anyway.'

'Here, no, look . . .' He tried to stop her opening the door. After all, here it was well past midnight and if Sue got away what was he going to do for a bird?

'Goodnight, Morgan.' She was halfway out of the car.

'Sue . . .'

'It's been a lovely evening. Ring me sometime if you like.' The door was closing behind her and Morgan was lying across the seat clutching ineffectually at her with his left hand.

'No, Sue, don't go.'

''Night.' She had shut the door and was smiling in at him through the open window.

He made a final, desperate attempt. 'Don't you want to know who Henry's bird is?'

She stopped, very still, no longer smiling. 'Will you tell me?'

'Yeah. Get back in the car.'

'I'm not making any deals, you know,' she said, cautiously.
'All right but get back in the car.'
She hesitated. Then . . . 'Okay,' she said and got back in the car . . .
Granny's barman shouted: 'Last orders, gennulmen, please!'
Morgan said: 'Yeah, so I just ran her home, said goodnight and left her.'
Henry frowned. 'Must have been pretty late. I was trying to phone her all night and she wasn't in. What were you doing?'
'Nothing,' Morgan said. 'Nothing at all. Have the other half?'
'Thanks.'
Morgan got the drinks and said: 'Anyway, you're all right. She kept on trying to pump me about you and that bird but I just said "Sorry, darlin', no can do." Well, it wasn't on, was it?'
'Good old Morgan,' Henry said. 'You're a real pal.'

20. 'ARE YOU IN OR OUT?'

There had been a storm just before lunch but it had passed away by the time Henry and Morgan left the pub. The afternoon was heavy and sultry and the smell of hot, wet dust hung around the streets.

'See you at the BBC,' Morgan said. 'About four.'

'Yes, all right.' Henry had not told him about the morning's events and the fact that his job was likely to be taken from him before the afternoon was out. Indeed, it had almost slipped his own mind in the excitement and anguish of hearing about Sue. Morgan's story had worried him quite a lot because there was so little detail in it and after they had parted – each to return to his office – he wished he had questioned Morgan more closely.

What else had the pair of them talked about over dinner or in the car, apart from the question of whom Henry was sleeping with? Morgan had been very elusive on these matters and it was most disturbing. Not, of course, that it really concerned Henry any more at all. His life with Sue was over; rather abruptly, perhaps, but over nonetheless.

When he considered it, the speed at which it had all taken place still astonished him and he thought what had happened was that all the glory of suddenly being a successful writer had gone to Sue's head. Delusions of adequacy. Her pride had been hurt by Henry's escapade with the Jungle Bunny and this new-born arrogance had forbidden her to forgive him. No doubt she thought he would soon be around begging her to take him back. Well, if so she was wron

He had given up begging. He had given up letting people kick him around and trample on him when he was down. Surely the way he had stood up to Coughlin this morning had proved that. A new Henry Tyson had arisen, older, harder, battle-scarred.

Sue had left him. Well, all right, okay. If that was the way she wanted it, so let it be. His extra-marital caper was only an excuse anyway. Quite obviously Sue had wanted to be rid of him before that and had seized upon this solitary lapse of his as the ideal opportunity to go.

The beer he had drunk and the surly heat of the afternoon combined to induce a peculiar mood in him. He was a long way short of drunk and yet he was hung over. He felt excited and nervous. He was taut and irritable. His temper was short and his head was aching.

If Sue wanted a divorce, okay, she could have one. He was not the kind of man to hang around where he wasn't wanted. He had his pride, by Golly. But there was just one thing she'd better know: there was to be no funny business about Timmy. Henry had not perhaps been the most attentive father in the world but he loved his son deeply and he'd better bloody well be given a damn sight more than just reasonable access to him or else.

In which pugnacious frame of mind he phoned Sue again and there was still no answer.

Bitch! Where was she? Out somewhere, he supposed, throwing her pants over the windmill to celebrate her newly acquired freedom.

He put the phone down and beckoned sharply to the copy boy with the Dirty Jug to pour him some tea.

'What time are you seeing Coughlin?' Bilbow asked. He was very piqued because he knew something serious was going on and Henry wouldn't tell him what it was.

Henry looked at the newsroom clock. 'Right now.'

'Bad, is it?'

'Bad enough. I think he *is* going to fire me.'

'No!' Bilbow leaned forward, eyes shining like a pair of glow-worms. 'What for?'

'I can't explain now. I expect he's waiting for me.' Henry put his cup down and hurried away.

Bilbow shouted after him. 'I say! You won't go and kill yourself before you've told me what he says, will you?'

Henry tapped lightly on Coughlin's door. Under normal circumstances he would have walked straight in but today was hardly normal so he knocked and waited.

'Yes.'

He went in. Coughlin was alone at his desk, smoking a cigarette, which was unusual because Henry had never known him to smoke before. He glanced up in a preoccupied way as Henry came in bristling and defensive and all strung-up for the verbal battle that was about to commence.

'Yes?'

'You wanted to see me.'

'Did I?' Coughlin frowned vaguely. He kept directing apprehensive looks at the telephone as if he expected it to leap from the desk and attack him. 'Yes, that's right, I did.'

He fell silent. Henry was silent, too. It was very quiet in the room with just the two of them hanging about saying nothing.

'Well?' Henry said at last.

'Yes.' Coughlin put out his cigarette and lit another one. 'You can go now,' he said.

'Pardon?' Henry was astonished.

'You can go. I haven't time to see you now. I'll call you in when I want you.'

'Well, but . . .'

The phone rang with an abruptness that startled them both. Coughlin's hand reached out with remarkable speed and plucked the receiver from its rest. 'Yes, sir. Yes, sir. Yes . . . Well, yes, I . . .'

The voice at the other end was clearly very angry. From where Henry stood, though, the words were indistinguishable, like the sound of distant barking.

'Woof, woof, woof, woof! Woof?'

'No, sir, but if I may . . .' Coughlin's face was tight and there was sweat on his forehead. Angrily he gestured to Henry to go.

'Woof, woof, woof, woof, woof!'

'I know that now, sir. I . . . I realize . . .'

'Woof, woof, woof!!'

'Well, you see, sir, I wasn't aware . . .'

'Woof! Woof, woof?'

'But, sir, you must see my position . . .'

Henry closed the door behind him as Coughlin's secretary came along the passage. 'He's on the phone,' he said. 'I think it's private.'

'Oh? Who's he talking to?'

'I don't know. It sounded like a very old Doberman Pinscher.'

The girl pursed her lips. 'That'll be the chairman. Mr Coughlin's been in all lunch-time waiting for him to call.'

'Oh? What about?'

'I don't know but it's something big.' She eased the door open and went inside.

Henry returned to his desk.

'Well?' Bilbow said. 'Are you in or out?'

'I've no idea. He was too busy to talk to me.'

'Tut.' Bilbow said. 'How very annoying.' He looked annoyed, too, for the doubt surrounding Henry's future was weighing heavily on his nerves. 'It's too bad of him, keeping one in suspense like that.'

'I'm sorry it's upsetting you,' Henry said, mildly. He picked up the phone again and dialled but the Jungle Bunny wasn't in, either.

Obviously she hadn't got back from her audition yet. He thought, guiltily, that he really knew very little about this girl with whom he was apparently going to make his life. He didn't even know the name of the show she was trying for, or where the audition was being held. With a sigh he replaced the receiver and began to read the latest cricket scores in the *Evening Standard.*

The afternoon passed quietly. Nobody bothered him, Coughlin didn't call for him, the news editor gave him no work to do and even Bilbow was too busy to talk to him. Henry read the evening papers and a couple of magazines, made an abortive attempt at the *Times* crossword puzzle and finally, just before six, got through to the Jungle Bunny.

'How'd you get on?' he asked.

'They said I'm not to call them; they'll call me.'

'Oh. Bad luck.'

'That's the way it goes,' she said wearily. 'How about you?'

'Well,' he said, 'I've been thinking that perhaps I'd better go back to my house tonight. I want to make sure everything's all right and I've got to collect my clothes and things.'

'Okay. You'll stay there will you?'

'I might as well. Just for tonight.'

'Yes, all right.'

'You don't mind?' he said anxiously.

'No, why should I?'

It seemed to Henry that there ought to be lots of reasons why she should mind but he couldn't think how to put them into words, so he merely said: 'Well, I'll see you tomorrow then. Can we have lunch together?'

'Why not? Give me a ring, about elevenish.'

'Yes. All right.'

And that was that. It left him feeling dissatisfied and irritable. Why did she have to be so goddam cool all the time? Why couldn't she inject a little passion into their relationship?

Damn her, he thought. Damn all women.

At six o'clock he went to get his car. A female traffic warden was strolling away up the street and there was a parking ticket attached to his windscreen.

21. HOME AGAIN

Among the rows of almost identical little homes Henry's stood out defiantly as the only one with recognizable character, if only because it had about it no gnomes or artificial wishing wells and the grass in the front garden was knee high.

He put the car in the garage and stopped for a moment on the verge of the wilderness. Before and on either side of him stretched neat little plots with neat little lawns and neat little flower-beds, all tended, he thought without rancour or envy, by neat little men with neat little lives.

He looked around to see if anyone he knew was still about but the road and the gardens were deserted. The rain clouds had gathered again and besides it was seven o'clock and all his neighbours would be indoors watching television.

Maybe that was what he would do, he thought, as he opened the front door – just sit back and watch TV all night. He had not done that for ages because he had not had the chance. This would be the first night he had spent alone and with nothing to do for months, and it came to him that the ideal situation he had outlined to Morgan had arisen: marriage had been switched off and he was free to watch TV or write a sonnet or get drunk or . . .

He stood in the silent, deserted hallway feeling very depressed.

Memories of the switched-off marriage were all around him – in the striped wallpaper and the burgundy carpet; in the Lowry print on the wall and the tiny red gum-boots under the coat rack; in the very air and the light smell upon it that was neither pleasant nor unpleasant but was simply the very special smell of this house, his house, the house where he had lived with his wife and his son. No other house in the world smelled quite like that and no other house in the world ever would.

He wished, desperately, that his marriage had never been switched off or, alternatively, that he could switch it on again. If only he could open the door to the dinette and find Sue sitting there. He wouldn't say anything. He would just walk up to her, kiss her, hug her. Probably he would cry a bit; probably she would, too, for they both became wet-eyed in emotional moments. Then, still holding her, he would apologize . . . 'I'm sorry. Oh, darling, I'm sorry. Forgive me . . .'

He went into the dinette. Sue was sitting at the table, sewing buttons on one of Timmy's little shirts. Henry stopped, very still, and looked at her and she looked at him, the shirt in one hand, the poised needle in the other.

'Oh, hullo,' he said. 'You're back then?'

The needle continued on its way, through the button and the shirt and then back again from the other side.

'Yes.'

His eyes on the quick, fluent movements of her hand, he said: 'I didn't expect to find you here.'

'No, I suppose not. I didn't expect to see you.'

'No, I suppose not.'

She bent forward and her hair fell silkily against her face as she bit through the cotton. 'Are *you* back then?'

'No,' he said. 'No, well, I just came to get some things.'

'Oh, I see. Yes.'

He scratched the nape of his neck and shuffled his feet, while Sue rethreaded the needle and started on another button.

'Well, I'll . . . I'll just go and pack then.'

'Yes, all right.'

He stood at the door. There were so many things he wanted to say and he couldn't think how to begin. He wanted, particularly, to say 'I love you' but after all that had gone before it seemed too startling an opening. Better, perhaps, to work up to that.

'Why did you walk out on me?' he asked.

She shrugged. 'Oh, well . . .' Her voice held no expression at all. 'Best thing, wasn't it?'

'It was the first time, you know.'

'What was?'

'That girl.'

'Oh, that.' Another shrug. Her head was still bent over the sewing and he stared at the slim, graceful line of her neck.

'What do you mean – oh, that? Isn't that what it's all about?'

'Don't shout,' she said, without looking up.

'I'm not bloody shouting,' he shouted. 'Christ Almighty, you walk out without giving me a chance to explain and now when I come in and try to talk to you all you can say is "Oh, that" . . .'

'If you must shout, close the door,' she said. 'Timmy's asleep upstairs.'

'Oh, God!' He gave the door a savage kick and it slammed behind him. Sue shook her head ever so slightly, ever so sadly, in that resigned, infuriating, totally feminine way. Henry turned from her, fumbling with clumsy hands for his cigarettes.

When he had lit up and sucked away for a second or two, he said: 'Well. It doesn't matter, anyway. Any excuse would have done, wouldn't it? You just wanted to be rid of me.'

'I did it,' she said, slowly and calmly, 'because it was the best thing for you.'

He stared at her. 'For me? For *me*?'

'Yes. Because we hadn't been getting along together, because you were restless and unhappy and . . . and resentful of me and because, oh, because you obviously didn't want to be married to me any more.'

He let out a curious sound that might have been a laugh or on the other hand might not. 'You're mad. Look, I know what I did was wrong and I'm deeply sorry for it but . . .'

Sue put the shirt down on the table and carefully replaced the needle in her workbasket. She said: 'That wasn't important. That kind of thing isn't the cause of a marriage break-up, it's only a symptom.'

'Don't quote the Marriage Guidance Council at me! Causes, symptoms – I don't know what you're talking about. All I know is that I went off the tracks once, just once, and you didn't care enough to understand, to forgive, even to ask for an explanation. And now you tell me you walked out for *my* sake, because *I* didn't want to be married. Well, I *mean*!'

Henry's temper had long gone and now Sue's flew away to join it. 'Well, for God's sake, it wasn't me who went off and slept with the bloody girl!'

'No, and why did I do it, eh? Because you weren't there, because you couldn't be bothered, that's why. It wouldn't have happened if you'd been there!'

'Well, I should hope not!'

They stood toe to toe in the middle of the room, their faces thrust pugnaciously towards each other, and in a silence broken only by the sound of irate breathing they held this eyeball to eyeball confrontation for a moment or two longer. Then Henry turned away to put out his cigarette.

'I was fed up,' he said, more quietly. 'Fed up. Everywhere I turned women were dominating my life, taking my job, arranging my free time . . . I'd had enough.'

'Oh, God,' said Sue, histrionically, 'the women-are-taking-over bit. And after that, I suppose, we'll have the poor-old-man-of-thirty-five bit. Oh, the self-pity!'

'Belt up. You don't even try to understand.'

'Quite right, I don't. Here you are with all these women messing you about – so you say – and the first thing you do is nip smartly off to bed with yet another woman. What kind of an answer was that?'

'I was lonely,' he said.

'Lonely!'

'Yes! It's a lonely business slogging your guts out trying to make a living.' (The principle of the thing, he felt, was accurate, although in truth his own guts were quite a long way from being slogged out.) 'Particularly when your wife is so busy with books and publishers and parties that she can't spare one lousy evening of her valuable time to take an interest in what her husband's doing. My God, these last few months I've been hanging around like the spare whatsit at the wedding.'

'Well, for heaven's sake!' She stood facing him, hands on hips, feet apart, face flushed and very pretty. 'You think I did all these things just for fun? I did it for *us*. You think it was any great pleasure looking after Timmy and the home all day long and then working at a drawing-board and a typewriter all night?'

They were both shouting again.

'Well, what fun do you think I had?' he yelled. 'Working in the office all day and then coming home at night and cooking and washing up and getting a rash all over my hands?'

'I cook and wash up all day long!'

'And I do it all bloody night!'

More heavy breathing; more silence. Like boxers slugging it

out they seemed to require a minute's respite now and then to recoup their energies.

Sue said: 'You didn't have to.'

'No, I could have starved to death, I suppose.'

'You should have said!' An ominous tremble had crept into her voice and if she was attempting to control it she was having very little success. 'I didn't think you minded looking after yourself when I was busy. I'd have got a meal for you – if you'd asked.'

'I did ask. Once. It was like I'd interrupted Shakespeare in the middle of writing *Hamlet*.'

She glared at him, panting. And then she sniffed suddenly, the corners of her mouth drooped and a couple of enormous tears rolled slowly down her lower lashes and fell onto her cheeks.

'Oh, hell,' Henry said. Women always won. If they couldn't out-talk you they outwept you. 'I'll go and pack.'

He had reached the door and was on the point of opening it when she spoke again in a voice that was damp and full of sniffles. 'If you leave this house now . . .' a quavering gulp and a heavy swallow . . . 'it'll be the end.'

He turned slowly. 'What do you mean – the end? I thought we were already doing the epilogue.'

She carried on snuffling quietly into her handkerchief. 'You know what I mean. If you go now, back to that woman, you needn't ever come back here, not ever.'

Henry watched her solemnly. Most women grew red-eyed and puffy when they cried but Sue somehow managed to escape that. All that happened when she wept was that her eyes shone and her cheeks grew slightly pale and she looked achingly lost and forlorn and he thought it was pretty rotten of her. Why couldn't she look ugly like any other girl?

'Do you want me to stay?' he asked.

The question provoked another onslaught of shoulder heaving and curious muffled sounds uttered into the handkerchief. 'You wouldn't ask that if you loved me. You wouldn't need to. You'd *want* to stay. But you don't love me. You've never loved me.'

Now was his opportunity, the moment for the declaration he had wanted to make before the rowing and the weeping began. He took a deep breath and prepared to deliver his tender message.

' 'Course I bloody love you!' he roared. Oh God, it had all come out wrong.

She looked up, blinked twice, swallowed . . . 'Wah!' she said.

Clumsily he went to her, patting her on the shoulder, murmuring 'There, there' and 'Now, now' but it did no good. A woman who has made up her mind to cry is not easily dissuaded from such a course.

'I'll make some tea,' he said at length.

When he came back it was over. The tears had stopped and it was as if she had never wept in her life. They sat opposite each other at the table sipping tea like two polite children at a party.

'How's Timmy?' Henry asked.

'He's fine. He missed you.'

'I missed him.' He made an instant resolution to spend more time with Timmy in future.

They were silent again for a little while, an awkward silence, lumpy with embarrassment.

'That woman,' Sue said. 'That girl you . . .'

'Leave it, Sue,' he said, gently.

'No, I don't want to know what you *did*. I just want . . .'

'Leave it.'

'I just want to know what you said to her, that's all.'

'Look, it's over now. Let it rest.'

'No, but . . .'

'It's over.'

Another silence, heavier even than its predecessor.

'Was she pretty?'

'Look . . .'

'Well, was she?'

'I don't see any point in discussing this.'

'Wasshepretty?' The words rushed out in a heap as if she feared that a gag was about to be forcibly applied to her mouth and it was essential for her to ask this vital question before such a calamity occurred. 'Wassheprettierthanme? Wasshe?'

'Sue . . .'

'And what did you say to her? I want to know what you *said* to her!'

Henry got up slowly, as one who had grown infinitely weary. 'I'm sorry but I can't stand this.'

'Did you tell her you loved her?' It was not so much a question as a wail of anguish, a cry for reassurance. 'What did you *say* to her?'

'I don't want to discuss it.' He stopped by the door, looking back at her gloomily.

'But you must!' she said. 'We've got to have it out. I've got to know if you said the same things to her that you say to me. I've got to know where I stand!'

'You know where you stand. I'm here. I'm back. I've made my choice.' It sounded so arrogant like that. Look, girls, Sue's got Henry back! Lucky, lucky Sue.

'Just tell me!' Her clenched fists rested on the table, tight and hard like little rocks.

Henry nodded, sighed. 'I see. I thought it was too easy. I thought I was forgiven but I'm not, am I? I've got to squirm and feel a little pain before you even begin to forgive me. Well, I don't think I'll wait around for that. I don't think it's worth it. Goodbye, Sue.'

She got to the front door just as he was about to open it. 'Where are you going?'

'Where do you think?' His hand was on the latch and her hand was on his, holding him. They stared at each other and there was no anger in either of them now. After a little while she let him go.

'All right. If it's what you want.'

'I've got to.' The great cliché of all the Western movies – a man's gotta do what a man's gotta do. Well, it was true enough. He didn't want to return to Sue on her terms nor even, indeed, on his own terms. He had to return on equal terms, both of them starting afresh with mutual understanding, or there was no hope for him. Sue had too much power in their marriage already; he couldn't afford to give her more. 'Don't you see?'

'No, I don't.' The tremble was back in her voice. 'You said you loved me but . . .'

He smiled gently. 'That's right. I love you. But.'

And at that moment there was a very loud knock on the door.

22. MORGAN AGAIN

The sound startled them both.

'Who's that?' said Sue, wide-eyed and whispering.

'I've no idea. I suggest we open the door and find out.' Whereupon, like the man of action he was, Henry opened the door to disclose the figure of Morgan waiting on the doorstep.

'Christ! Henry.' Morgan's sharp, salesman's gaze alighted first, furtively, on Henry, flickered across to Sue and back to Henry. 'Oh, hello, Henry, darlin'. Come to see you, haven't I?'

'Have you?' Henry asked, curtly. There were times when he was glad to see Morgan and there were times when he wasn't and this was undeniably one of the latter occasions. Unfortunate, but that was the way it went.

'Yes. Hello, Sue.'

'Hello, Morgan.'

The gaze flickered about again, never quite catching anyone's eye. 'It's my old woman,' Morgan said. 'She's left me.' There was a note of genuine grievance in his voice. 'Just like that. Run off with the geezer next door.'

Clouds had been building up slowly since the late afternoon and now it had begun to rain, not tempestuously as at lunch time, but in a steady, persistent drizzle.

'You've come all this way,' Henry said, 'to tell me that?'

'Yeah. Well,' Morgan shuffled about on the doorstep, 'I had to tell someone, didn't I?'

'I'm very sorry, Morgan,' Sue said, quietly.

'Yeah. Bloody mare.' Morgan looked up at the rain and brushed a few drops from his coat. 'Can I come in?'

Henry hesitated. 'I'm just leaving,' he said.

'Oh, well.' Morgan at once began to look more cheerful. 'Don't let me stop you. I'll just stay here for a bit and talk to Sue. Helps to talk to someone.'

'You can talk to me,' Henry said, 'on the way back to Town. You can give me a lift.'

'Hey, no, hang on. I've only just got here.'

'Yes, and now you're leaving. Come on.' Henry stepped out and joined him in the rain.

'Henry,' Sue called sharply. 'Henry, don't . . .'

'I'll leave the car with you,' he said. 'Goodbye, Sue.' He took Morgan by the arm and led him quickly down the path.

'Bit bloody rotten,' Morgan said, grumpily. 'Come all this bleedin' way and don't get offered so much as a cup of tea.'

Henry said nothing. He sat in the front of Morgan's car and stared ahead through the windscreen, not looking back, though he knew Sue was still in the doorway, watching them. Morgan put the car into gear and they lurched and roared up the road and round the corner and away from the little house and the still, blonde figure standing on the doorstep as motionless as any ornamental gnome.

'You're a bloody liar,' Henry said.

'Do what?' Morgan said, affronted.

'You didn't come to see me at all. You came rutting round after Sue, didn't you? You had no idea I'd be there. What a lousy bastard you are.'

'That's a rotten thing to say,' Morgan said.

'It was a rotten thing to do.' The rain had begun lashing down and the windscreen wiper on Henry's side had stopped working. He saw everything as through a waterfall, distorted and unreal. 'Has your wife really left you?'

'Yeah. Well, I'd not been home for a few nights and when I did get back this evening, I found this note propped up against the Busy Lizzie. My old woman . . .' Morgan shook his head in wonderment at the perfidy of women. 'What a cow. She'd been having it away with the feller next door for months. Nice bastard he must be, too. Left a wife and four kids.'

Henry tutted in sympathy. 'Some people,' he said, innocently, 'have no conception of their marital responsibilities.'

'Bloody right,' said Morgan. He drove slowly through Regent's Park, peering through the steam that formed and was wiped away and instantly reformed on the inside of the windscreen.

'I expect you're very upset,' Henry said.

'No. I'm not – the woman next door is, though. Crying her eyes out she was when I left.'

'I should have thought,' Henry murmured, 'that instead of shooting round to make a pass at Sue, you'd have been better off commiserating with your poor, abandoned neighbour.'

The car turned into the top of Regent Street and inched along with the rest of the traffic towards Oxford Circus.

'Yeah. Well, I would have stayed only I didn't fancy her much.'

'Quite,' Henry said. 'Silly of me not to think of that.'

'So I came out to your place,' Morgan said. 'I wanted someone to talk to, really, that's all. Just someone to talk to. Funny, that.'

Past the traffic lights, down Regent Street towards Piccadilly.

'Where can I drop you?' Morgan asked.

'Granny's. I left my raincoat there at lunchtime.'

Down the Haymarket, left to Charing Cross, along the Strand and around the Aldwych to Fleet Street.

'So that's two of us with our marriages gone for a Burton,' Morgan said.

'Looks like it.' Henry's tone was decidedly short because, in this instance, he didn't much like to equate himself with Morgan.

'Best thing, probably,' Morgan said. 'I never was all that keen on marriage.' He paused at the pedestrian crossing by the Law Courts to yell foul things at an old man who was taking his time about limping across the road. 'Hey, I've just had a marvellous idea – why don't we share a pad, you and me?'

'Well...'

'It'd be great! Here, tell you what – why not bring that Jungle Bunny in with us? We could share her and all.'

He stopped the car outside Granny's and turned towards Henry a face that shone with the excitement of his marvellous idea. 'What do you reckon? We can always have other birds, too, of course.'

Henry stared thoughtfully at the rain. 'I think it's a horrible idea,' he said.

'What?'

'And I'll tell you something else. If I hear you've been sniffing around Sue again, I'll cite you as co-respondent.'

Morgan stopped looking excited and gazed at him instead in disbelief. 'Co-refuckinspondent!' he said. 'Co-re . . . You *must* be joking! If anyone does any divorcing there, darlin', it'll be Sue divorcing you.'

'Then I'll cross-petition,' Henry said, calmly. 'I'll drag you into it somehow.'

Morgan was silent, doubtless thinking it over. 'Got a fag?' he said. Henry gave him one. 'Ta.' He wound down the window and blew smoke into the street. 'You know, you want to grow up, Henry mate. If Sue's kicked you out it's your own fault and if she wants to shack up with someone else, she's got every right.'

'Quite so,' Henry said.

'So there's no point in being dog-in-the-mangerish about it.'

'Exactly.'

'You see what I mean then?'

'Yes. And if I catch you sniffing around Sue again I'll cite you as co-respondent.' Henry buttoned his jacket. 'Fancy a drink?'

Morgan considered it and decided to decline. 'No, thanks. I think I'll be off.'

'Where?'

'Oh, I'm not schlapping all the way back to your house, don't worry. Anyway, I don't think Sue fancies me much. I had a go there last night, matter of fact, but she wasn't having any. Pity really. No, I think I'll go and fetch that blonde I met at the Golden Circle. Right little raver, she was.'

Henry got out of the car. 'Aren't you going to look for your wife?' he asked.

'No. What for? Bugger her.' With a light-hearted wave, Morgan was gone, another lonely man in search of company.

23. SCENES FROM DOMESTIC LIFE . . . 3

'I remember, I remember . . .'

A bright summer's morning, the sun and the birds already up and doing, and the scent of roses drifting into the bedroom.

Sue, shaking him by the arm, woke Henry up.

'Henry! Henry!'

'Wha . . . ? Huh? Ergh? Wassamatter?'

'Was that your alarm clock not going off?'

They both lay still and listened.

'Probably,' he said. 'I've been lying here listening to it not go off all night. Hark, there it doesn't go again!'

'No,' she said, giggling, 'but you know what I mean. I heard it twiddle.'

'Twiddle?'

'Yes. You know – the sort of twiddly noise it makes when you think it's going to go off but doesn't.'

He pulled her on top of him and nibbled gently at the tip of her nose. 'That's a good Zen question actually. You know the sound of an alarm clock going off? Well, what's the sound of an alarm clock not going off?'

'Ass! What time is it anyway?'

He consulted the clock. 'It'll continue not going off for the next half hour. There's plenty of time.'

She drew back, squinting at him suspiciously. 'What for?'

'You know what for?'

'Oh, do I?'

'Yes, you do.'

From a distance of about six inches she studied his face gravely. Then she smiled. 'I love you.'

'I love you too.'

'Isn't it nice?'

'Yes.'

'Shut the door, then.'

'All right, then.'

He was sitting in the lounge with Timmy beside him and reading aloud a chapter from *The House at Pooh Corner* and Sue was dashing to and fro in one of her flaps.

He was conscious of her voice, chattering to him, as she bustled about the house, first in their bedroom, then in Timmy's, then trailing through the lounge and into the kitchen and from there to the dinette and all the way back again. He had the peculiar impression that she was moving faster than sound for often her voice seemed to come from the room she had just left . . .

'Gosh, I don't know how I'm going to get through the day, I really don't. So much to *do*! Oh, God where did that child leave his shoes? Timmy, where are your . . .? Oh, here they are, right underneath the lavatory. And the shopping! What do you fancy for dinner? How about lamb cho . . . Oh, Lord, and then I've got to see Lorna Collins about the Residents' Association and the car has to go in for a service and . . .'

Henry deeply enjoyed these moments. He liked reading to his son and he liked Winnie the Pooh and he liked seeing his wife fitting occasionally into the role of harrassed, scatter-brained little woman. He carried on listening and reading.

'. . . and the publishers want me to rewrite that chapter before the end of the week and . . . God, that boy's put his socks in the butter dish again. I don't know *what* I'm going to do with him, I really don't. Oh, and I've got to take old Mrs Hollis to the station. Poor old dear can't walk more than a few yards and her children never come to see her. I think it's a shame . . . And, oh, hell, look at the time!'

She loomed up suddenly before her husband and son with a wet flannel in her hand and before Henry could move she had wiped it briskly around his face.

'. . . never get it all done, never' she said, despairingly.

'Hey! What are you . . . ? Get off!' Henry said, through the flannel.

She stopped wiping his face and flung her arms round his neck as a token of apology. 'Oh, darling, I *am* sorry. I thought it was Timmy . . . I . . . Oh, I've got so much on my mind, I don't know *what* I'm doing.'

'It's all right, I needed a bit of a wash anyway.'

Timmy, seeing the hated flannel approaching and taking advantage of the miracle by which it had missed him, had fled the room.

Henry clasped his wife by the hips. 'Calm down,' he said, kissing the crook of her elbow. 'Just take it easy for a bit. Come and sit on my lap.'

'I haven't got *time*!'

'Yes, you have?'

'Have I?'

'Certainly. Besides, you know you want to.'

'Do I?'

'Yes, you do.'

'All right, then.'

Sue leaned over the banisters and called down to him in the hall.

'Darling, did you get the car back?'

'Yes.'

'Is it all right?'

'Fine, as far as I can tell. They did the full 6,000 – mile service.'

She started coming down the stairs, in a hurry as usual. 'Yes, I know but did they twiddle the whatsit?'

'Eh?'

'The whatsit,' she said impatiently. '*You* know. Did they twiddle it?'

'Ah,' he said. 'Ah, well there you have me. I wasn't vouchsafed this information. The man at the garage doesn't like discussing these matters with me because he knows I don't understand that kind of technical language.'

Against her will, she started to laugh. 'You know what I mean.'

'Yes, I know and I'm sure the whatsit has been twiddled as firmly as any purist could wish and has anyone ever told you that you're a bit of a half-wit?'

'Am I?' she said, standing close to him.

'Yes, you are.'

'Kiss me, then.'

'All right, then.'

24. BILBOW'S TALE

Henry's coat was hanging on the peg beside the fireplace where he had left it at lunchtime and Bilbow, shirt-sleeved and waving a pint of bitter about, was standing by the bar, roaring happily.

'Henry, c'mere!' His eyes were shining with joy and good-natured malice. 'Wotchergonave?'

'Pint of the best.'

'Pint of ordinary, my love,' Bilbow called to a nineteen-year-old barmaid with a thirty-year-old bust. It was his contention that ordinary bitter was perfectly as good as best bitter – better even. It was also cheaper and for these two excellent reasons he never bought anything but ordinary, either for himself or anyone else.

'Missed a lot of excitement tonight, kid,' he said, handing Henry a tankard. Much of his own beer appeared to have been absorbed into his shirt front, as though he had been trying to feed it into himself through his navel. He didn't seem to mind, though, partly no doubt because he was rather drunk.

Henry looked at his watch. He was anxious to get away, not being in the mood for boozing it up with the boys. 'Oh?' he said. There were a lot of *Journal* men dotted around among the customers and he was afraid that if he stayed too long he would become inextricably involved in a drinking school that would end only at closing time when, swollen and smelly with beer, they would roll out into the street and belch and fart their way to the Press Club, there to begin all over again.

'Yes,' Bilbow said, 'hell of a lot of excitement.' He peered at Henry closely, savouring his moment of revelation like a conjuror who was about to astonish his audience by producing from his hat not the anticipated rabbit but an elephant. 'Coughlin's gone.'

Henry's glass stopped a few inches from his lips, his drinking arm paralysed with shock. 'Gone? What do you mean – gone?'

'Fired. Sacked. Booted out. Gone, gone and never called me mother.' Rather gracefully for so bulky a man, Bilbow hopped from one foot to the other and back and finished with an elegant little sideways kick with his right foot. The manoeuvre pleased him so much that he did it again.

'Why?' Henry said. 'He can't have been fired. He's too well in with the chairman.'

'*Was*, old kid, *was*. Now he's well out with the chairman because what old Coughlin didn't know was . . .' Bilbow drank deeply of his beer and put his glass down. 'My old friend here,' he said to the barmaid, 'wishes to buy me a pint of ordinary, don't you, old friend?'

'Yes, yes,' Henry said, scattering coins on the bar. 'Go on.'

'Well, Coughlin takes on Mark Payne, right? Column a week for a year, eighty quid a time.'

'Mark told me a hundred,' Henry said.

'No, eighty, take my word for it. Anyway, no contract drawn up but as good as because old Coughlin makes the offer in writing and Payne writes back accepting, right?'

'Yes and for Christ's sake get on with it.'

'All right. All right.' Bilbow took another long, noisy gulp of beer. 'Anyway, Coughlin gets Payne's letter – just before lunch-time this must have been – takes it up to the chairman and says "There, sir, look, sir, what a bright boy I've been, sir," and the chairman takes one look and practically *craps* himself with rage.'

'Why?' Henry's glass stood, forgotten, on the bar and Bilbow, who never liked to see beer go flat for want of someone to drink it, confiscated it for himself.

'Because . . .' and here Bilbow paused a while to focus more intently on Henry's face . . . 'Payne's been screwing the chairman's daughter-in-law.'

Henry was aware that his mouth was hanging open. 'What?' he said.

'Payne's been screwing . . .'

'Blonde girl, model? Drives a Thunderbird?'

'Very likely. Do you know her? Bilbow asked curiously.

'She was in here the other day to collect Mark after lunch. Upstairs. Coughlin was there, too.'

'Didn't he know who she was?'

'No. He asked me. I didn't know either – then. Good God.' He remembered how anxious the girl had been to leave the pub and indeed the district and also what Mark had said about her later at the Puking Cat. If, of course, it was the same girl. Yes, of course, it was the same girl. Even Mark would hardly be conducting affairs with two married women simultaneously.

'Been going on for ages apparently,' Bilbow said, with great satisfaction, 'though I gather the chairman and, come to that, his son only heard about it in the last day or two.'

'The son,' Henry said. 'That's Kenneth, is it?'

'That's it. Kenneth Golt, MP. A right twat. Anyway, when he finds he's got the man who's cuckolding his son on the payroll, the chairman kicks Coughlin out of his office, has a fit, calls him back this afternoon and fires him. Two years' money, Coughlin got. And what makes it so pissingly funny is that on account of the letters that had gone back and forth, the old man had to pay Payne off with a year's salary, as well.'

'Mark's fired, too, then?'

'Not half. Jammy bugger though. Four thousand quid he's got and hasn't written a line.' Bilbow found this so hilarious that he had to clutch hold of the bar while he laughed.

'Where did you learn all this?' Henry asked.

'Usual sources.'

'I see.' It would be authentic then, for Bilbow was a great man for chatting up secretaries, particularly the editor's, a sharp, inquisitive woman who knew everything that happened within the *Journal* building and kept her friend Bilbow liberally supplied with accurate and confidential information.

'Well,' Henry said and was interrupted by an influx of eager *Journal* men who arrived with cries of, 'There's the man! He knows all about it,' and clustered around, faces avid for scandal, hands clinking coins, waving notes, shoulders jostling for a position next to the man who knew all about it.

'Wotchergonave, Bilbow?'

'Yes, wotchergonave, Billers?'

'Wotchergonave, Henry?'

'Wotchergonave . . . wotchergonave . . .?'

Henry withdrew from the crush and stole away. At the door he stopped and looked back. Bilbow, gloriously surrounded by pints of bitter, face shining and red, his shirt burst open and his belly showing pallid and hairy was staring after him.

'One thing,' he said. 'You won't get fired now, kid.'

Yes, that was true. With Coughlin gone, he was safe. And yet he didn't seem to care any more. He felt numb and emotionally giddy and it worried him rather because he ought to be experiencing sharper sensations. When he thought of Sue and Timmy he felt remorse and regret but only as a kind of ache instead of the acute and genuine pain he expected.

In an odd way, pity for Mark was as strong as any of his other emotions and that was absurd because, for all that had happened, Mark was still a great deal better off, richer and more successful, than he was. Even Mark's personal life, mess though it apparently was, could hardly be more tangled and depressing than Henry's own. Yet he felt sadder for Mark than he did for himself. A defence mechanism probably, he thought. Nature's way of protecting the open wounds.

He took a Tube from Blackfriars to Earl's Court and walked along the road to the house where the Jungle Bunny lived. The front door was open and he let himself in.

Already familiarity had bred acceptance of the place. He no longer noticed the curiously sexy smell of woman that hung around the hallway, or the dust on the stairs or the dirt on the walls.

His feet clattered on the worn linoleum as he ran up the last flight of stairs and banged on the Jungle Bunny's door. He was hungry now, not only for food but for her, too. His nerves seemed to have turned into springs tightly coiled within him and he was trembling with a purely animal excitement. There was no affection involved, he admitted to himself as he thumped the door again. All he wanted was release and oblivion.

He knocked for a third time and still nobody came to the door.

He reached up and felt above the lintel. His fingers dislodged dust and the shrivelled corpses of flies and finally came to the key.

When he opened the door the flat was dark and empty. There was a crumpled dress on the bed and one wedge-heeled shoe on the chair. In the kitchen the eyelashes still wilted on the window sill and the egg-encrusted plate had been removed and replaced by another on which bacon rinds lay in pools of solid fat like worms in aspic.

Henry's hunger weakened and died. If he was to continue living here, something would have to be done about cleaning the place, not just once in a while but regularly. It was strange that a girl so personally clean should be so careless about the state of her surroundings.

He made himself a cup of coffee and sat on the bed to drink it. It was half-past ten. He hoped the Jungle Bunny would be back soon, for though he no longer wanted food, he still wanted her. Or someone, anyway. Someone warm and soft to cuddle up close to and give him something else to think about than his personal miseries. For his mood was changing fast and feeling was coming back. Spasms of anguish for Sue and grief over Timmy and pity for himself took it in turns to afflict him and sometimes they all hit him together and then he would groan and say 'Oh, God' and it was as much a prayer as anything.

He had just put his cup down and his cigarette out and said 'Oh, God' for the third time in five minutes when every light in the place went off and left him in total darkness.

25. UNEXPECTED GUESTS

At first he thought it was a power cut for the landing light had gone out, too, and the whole of the upper part of the house was black. But when he leaned over the banisters and looked round the bend in the stairs he could see the faint glimmer of a lamp on the next floor down.

So it was quite simple, really. All he had to do was put money in the electricity meter, which would have been perfectly easy if he had had any idea where the bloody meter was.

If only he could turn on the light, he could find it, But, on the other hand, if he could turn on the light he wouldn't need to find it. His cigarette lighter gave him brief hope. The flame was weak but at least it provided some illumination, enough to least to help him find his way back into the flat. But that accomplished and satisfied that it had done a good job it wheezed out the last of its gas in one final flicker and died.

Henry put the lighter back in his pocket and began to grope his way around in search of the elusive electricity meter.

In the main room he barked his shin savagely against the chair and knocked it over beside the lamp. The shade fell off and he trod on it and heard it crackle and snap under foot. The base tumbled against his coffee cup, which rolled onto the bed and spilled its dregs over the sheets, and the saucer skidded onto the floor and shattered there.

The lampshade had worked its way around his ankle. Raging, he tore it off and flung it across the room and it landed on top of the chest of drawers amid the joyous tinkle of tumbling bottles. A strong sweet smell of perfume rose up and engulfed the room. Panicking, Henry stumbled across to the chest to repair the damage. He couldn't find the scent bottle but with appalling accuracy his fingers groped their way into cold cream and face powder, pools of hand lotion and little topless pots of rouge, mascara and God knew what.

'Oh, Christ!' he said and fled into the kitchen where the first thing he did was to knock the dirty plate into the sink. He picked the pieces up and put them back on the draining board but by now he had lost heart.

Sod the meter. Sod the Jungle Bunny. Sod Sue and Bilbow and Coughlin and Morgan. Sod everything.

He went back to the other room, found the bed and sat on the edge of it, his head in his hands. After a time he groaned and lay down and groaned again and in a little while, emotionally exhausted and lulled by the silence and the darkness, he fell asleep.

Some time later – how much later he had no idea – he was awakened by the sound of the door opening and the light switch clicking and nothing happening and the Jungle Bunny's voice saying 'Damn it!'

He struggled up, thick with sleep, as she moved into the room, sniffing sharply as the scent got to her. Then there was the scratching of a match and her disembodied head, black outlined against black, sprang into view.

'Hello,' said Henry.

'What? Oh, my God!'

'The lights went out,' Henry said.

At that moment another match was struck and just behind the Jungle Bunny, the large, sincere face of Mark Payne loomed up in the bright yellow flame.

'What the hell!' Henry said.

'Hello, Henry,' said Mark.

'Wait here,' said the Jungle Bunny. 'I'll put some money in the meter.'

She went into the kitchen, moving confidently in the darkness, leaving the two men alone. Mark's match went out and his face disappeared only to return immediately like a sincere Cheshire Cat, as he struck another one.

'What the devil are you doing here?' Henry demanded.

'I might ask you the same . . . aargh!' The match fell to the floor and conversation ceased while the sound of muffled cursing and finger sucking drifted across to the bed where Henry sat. After a moment, another match flared up. 'I might ask you the same thing,' Mark said.

'I live here!' Top that, Henry thought sourly.

Mark took in about a cubic yard of air through his nostrils and, turning the corners of his mouth down, looked as sincere as a man could be. 'That's all very well but you were supposed to be staying out tonight,' he said, with sharp reproach. 'If you ask me it's a pretty lousy trick, sneaking back like this to spy on the girl. What kind of a relationship are you going to have if you don't trust her?'

His face suddenly disappeared again.

'Hurry up with those lights!' Henry yelled into the kitchen. It was unnerving to sit there chatting to this incredible vanishing man.

'I'm trying to find some money!' the Jungle Bunny yelled back.

'Bloody hell!' All the frustrations, angers, griefs and worries of the past few days combined together to form one blood red spot of rage that burned fiercely in Henry's mind. He sprang up from the bed with the firm intention of smiting Mark Payne hip and thigh and just then the lights went on.

'Christ!' said the Jungle Bunny from the kitchen door. 'Look at the mess.' Then, as the full horror of the situation sank in, a rage equal to Henry's own blazed from her eyes. 'My make-up! My scent!' She rushed to the chest of drawers, scrabbling among the ruins she found there, and turned to glare at Henry. 'Look! My God, look at him! Look what the lunatic's done! He's painted himself with my bloody make-up!'

'What? Where?' Henry caught sight of himself in the mirror. His forehead and cheeks were daubed with eccentric streaks of mascara, rouge and face powder like war-paint applied by a Red Indian after a heavy night on the firewater.

'Blimey,' he said.

'Idiot! Lunatic! Bastard!' said the Jungle Bunny.

Mark Payne, no doubt in a misguided attempt to ease the tension in the room, gave forth a nervous laugh. It was an unwise move as it turned out, for both Henry and the Jungle Bunny turned their wrath on him.

'What are you laughing at?' the Jungle Bunny said.

'I'll kill him!' Henry said and resuming where he had left off when the lights came back he swung a huge punch in Mark's direction, missing by a considerable margin and reeling off-balance into the armchair. Undeterred he sprang up to have another go.

'Not on the face!' Mark shouted to him. 'Anywhere but the face! I'm on TV tomorrow . . .'

Henry leapt upon him and they wrestled impotently in the middle of the room. 'This isn't fair!' Mark said. 'You're breathing on my glasses . . .'

Not deigning to reply Henry tried to butt him in the mouth and missed and Mark tried to bite Henry's ear but got his coat collar instead. Then Henry brought his knee up with the shrewd intention of jabbing it into Mark's groin but as Mark had had precisely the same idea at precisely the same moment their knee-caps cracked sharply together and with little cries of pain they staggered apart.

'For God's sake, *stop* it,' said the Jungle Bunny.

The two men went to opposite sides of the room, rubbing their knees. 'Tell him to get out of here,' Henry said, sulkily.

She hesitated, looking from one to the other. 'Would you mind?' she said to Mark.

'Well . . . All right. I'll wait in the car.'

'Don't bother,' Henry said.

Mark glared at him from the door. 'I'll wait in the car,' he said again and then to the Jungle Bunny, just in case she hadn't grasped the point: 'I'll be waiting in the car.' He closed the door behind him in a dignified kind of way and they listened to his footsteps going down the stairs.

'You said you weren't coming back tonight,' the Jungle Bunny said. She went to the chest of drawers and tried to restore a little order.

'I changed my mind.' Henry tested his wounded knee a couple of times and, finding it still worked, sat down. 'How did you get lumbered with him, anyway?'

'I phoned him up.' She put the empty scent bottle back in its place. 'Look at that, at least three quid's worth of "Shocking" all soaked into this rotten carpet.'

'Why?'

'What do you mean – why?' she said angrily. 'You're the one who did it.'

'No, no. I mean, why did you phone him up?'

'Because he asked me to.' Carefully she scooped up a few ounces of face powder and put it back in the box. 'He gave me his number at the Puking Cat the other night. When we were dancing.'

'What kind of a man is he?' Henry asked, bitterly. 'He can't even be faithful to his mistress.'

'You weren't all that faithful to your wife.'

'That's different. You know it is.'

She shrugged. 'Why don't you wash that stuff off your face? It doesn't suit you, you know.'

'Very funny,' he jeered and went to the kitchen to get a damp cloth. 'I suppose,' he called from there, 'you're going to say you felt sorry for him, that he needs you?'

'Not at all,' she said. 'I need him. He can give me work on his show. That's why I called him up.'

Henry came back into the room, sneering. 'I see. So you just brought him back here to have a little business chat?'

'No,' she said, replacing the cap on the cold-cream jar, 'I brought him back here to sleep with me.'

'My God.' He sat down heavily on the bed. 'You admit that?'

'Why not?'

'But what about me?'

'I didn't think you'd be here.'

She took the damp cloth from him and wiped the chest of drawers. 'To tell you the truth, Henry, I didn't think you'd ever come back. I thought you'd stay with your wife.'

'You knew I wouldn't. That's all over.'

'Is it?'

'Of course. Sue and I just don't get on any more.'

'You love her, don't you?'

'What?' It was a hell of a question for a mistress, however fickle, to put to her lover and Henry paused before answering. 'Well, yes, I suppose I do,' he said. 'Loving someone is a habit, like smoking. It's not easy to give up, just like that. But our marriage is finished all the same. We don't communicate, that's our trouble. We talk but we don't communicate. There's a sort of . . . a sort of cotton wool curtain between us all the time. We talk to each other but nothing gets through.'

The Jungle Bunny went into the kitchen and began to brush her teeth with her customary ferocity. Henry padded along behind.

'So who does communicate these days?' she said, in a fine spray of toothpaste. 'Nobody. Except in bed. Life's too fast. Nobody's got time to communicate with anybody else. You talk and you make love and if a little understanding creeps in somewhere along the line, you're one of the lucky ones.'

Henry drew away from her. 'I don't want any of your basic philosophy, thank you very much,' he said, coldly.

She put her toothbrush away and returned to the other room. 'Unzip me, will you?' she said. 'And be careful this time.'

'Are we going to bed?'

'I'm going to bed with someone,' she said. 'But I haven't figured out who yet.'

'I've never met anyone like you.' There was a reluctant note of admiration in his voice.

She took her dress off and sat in front of the mirror to brush her hair. 'You're a funny boy. All you really want is someone to agree with you and feed your self-pity. That's the trouble with you, the trouble with your whole generation. You've got no guts.'

'What do you mean, my generation? It's the same generation as yours, more or less.'

'No it's not. Mine's a black generation. I'm an emergent Wog, remember?'

'Oh, shut up.'

He was cross with her and a little startled, too. 'If you feel like that, why did you take up with me?'

'Because I felt sorry for you.'

'*You* felt sorry for *me*?' he said.

She turned round and stared at him, her head propped on one hand. 'That's right. I may be just a Jungle Bunny to you but in many ways I'm a hell of a lot smarter than you are. You know your main trouble? Jealousy. You're dead jealous of your wife, because she's achieved something that you haven't.'

'You're mad,' he said. 'Right out of your mind. I told you what caused the trouble between Sue and me. We don't . . .'

'Oh, that's right,' she said, with scorn. 'You don't communicate, do you? Hah! I doubt if you've ever communicated with anyone in your life. It takes hard work, honeychile, and lots of practice and patience and you're too wrapped up in poor old Henry Tyson to bother about things like that.'

'I don't have to listen to this,' he said, haughtily.

'No, but you would if you had any sense . . . Where are you going?'

He had got up off the bed and was walking slowly towards the door. 'I've no idea. But I know where I'm not wanted.'

'Why don't you go home? Best place for you.'

He stopped walking and appealed to her in genuine anguish. 'Don't you mind if I go?'

'Not really. Oh, I do like you and you're fun to make love with, even though you're so innocent at it. But . . . oh, I don't know. We haven't a lot in common, really, have we?'

'I thought we had.'

'Well, we're both underdogs, there is that. Me, because I'm black and you because you chose to be one. That's why you fancied me, I think – one lame underdog teaming up with another. But you don't have to be an underdog, you know. It's up to you, really.'

'More bloody jungle philosophy,' he said, bitterly.

'I expect it is,' she agreed, unoffended. 'Don't make a noise as you go out.'

He stopped again. 'Is that it, then? All over?'

'I don't know. It depends on you. You can stay if you like, I don't mind, but you'll be a fool if you do. You ought to go home and make it up with your wife.'

'Look here,' he said, 'I . . .'

He was interrupted by a light tap on the door. Henry said: 'It's that bloody Mark Payne again'; the Jungle Bunny said: 'Come in'; and the door opened and Sue walked into the room.

26. CONFRONTATION

There was a lengthy period of silence that was only broken when Henry said 'Christ!' in an awed sort of voice.

Sue smiled dazzlingly upon him and came in a little further.

'I'm Henry's wife,' she said to the Jungle Bunny.

'Oh.' The girl got up. 'How do you do?'

They shook hands, making a nice contrast – Sue calm, blonde and wearing a sleeveless dress with a floral pattern; the Jungle Bunny understandably flustered, dark and wearing a white bra and pants.

'I seem to have arrived at an awkward moment,' Sue murmured, silkily. She gestured towards the crumpled bed. 'Or had you just finished?'

'No,' Henry said. 'No, Sue, it's not like that. Nothing's happened.' He had retreated into a corner where, watching the two women in his life, he had the unpleasant sensation that he was physically shrinking, becoming in every way more insignificant with each passing second.

The Jungle Bunny said: 'It's true, actually. Henry was just leaving. He was going home.'

'Was he?' Sue cast a grave eye over the crushed figure in the corner. Behind her, the Jungle Bunny was vigorously nodding 'Yes.'

'Yes,' Henry said.

'That's good,' Sue said, 'because I've come to take him home.'

The Jungle Bunny said, seriously, 'I'm glad. It's the best thing.'

'Oh?' Sue changed the grave look for a frosty one and gave the other girl the full benefit of it. 'Trying to get rid of him?'

'Oh, no, not at all. It's just that, well, I don't think he's very happy with me. I don't really know why he came here in the first place. You're the one he loves.'

'Now look here . . .' said the voice in the corner by way of protest but nobody seemed to hear him.

'Do you think so?' Sue said. 'That's just what I thought, too. That's why I came. You see, I shouldn't like to give him up, not without a struggle.'

To Henry, listening from the far side of the room, it all had a feeling of unreality. He might have been a much-valued butler that one society hostess had tried to steal from another and, most humiliating of all, the whole thing was being discussed on far too low an emotional key for his taste. A little weeping and shouting wouldn't have come amiss but, instead, even the very natural tension that had existed when Sue first arrived was diminishing fast and the conversation was taking on the tone of a cosy natter.

Sue and the Jungle Bunny were sizing each other up and in their mutual inspection there was no sign of hostility, merely the normal curiosity of two women who, temporarily anyway, were sharing the same man.

'I wondered what you'd be like,' Sue said. 'I thought you'd be different somehow.'

The Jungle Bunny nodded. 'Less black, I expect.'

'No, I knew you were black. I just thought you'd be, well, different, not so sort of English.'

'Yes, well, we don't all kill chickens on the carpet.' The Jungle Bunny hesitated. 'I thought you'd be different, too. Kind of grim and intellectual. Excuse me.' She found a housecoat of sorts and wrapped it round herself.

'I feel rather ashamed,' she said.

'Of being undressed?' Sue murmured, coolly. 'No need. I didn't think you and Henry had come up here for a prayer meeting.'

'No, I didn't mean that. It's just that I'm sorry to have been the cause of so much trouble between you and your husband. It's not much fun being the other woman, not when you meet the man's wife.'

Sue gave a little sigh. 'You weren't the cause,' she said. 'If it hadn't been you it would have been someone else. I think this kind of thing was bound to happen, sooner or later.'

'Yes, but I feel so awful about it, particularly being all naked like this. I mean, honestly, nothing has happened but . . . but it seems so cheap and nasty.'

'Never mind.' Sue gave her a gentle smile. 'I expect it was a bit unfair of me to come bursting in like that, playing the outraged wife.'

'Oh, but you're not!' said the Jungle Bunny. 'That's just it. I wouldn't feel so awful if you did!'

Henry looked on in sheer amazement. Good God, they'd be weeping on each other's shoulders next.

In fact, they did nothing of the kind. Instead the Jungle Bunny groped around on her dressing table and finding there a packet of Silk Cut offered one to Sue. 'Would you like a cigarette?'

'No, have one of mine.'

'No, no, I insist.'

'Oh, all right, then.' The pair of them lit up and blew smoke about.

'You've a little boy, haven't you?' said the Jungle Bunny.

'Yes. Timmy. He's four. Has Henry shown you a photograph?'

'No.'

'Hasn't he?' Sue directed a glance of reproach at her husband. 'Would you like to see one?' From her handbag she produced a picture which the Jungle Bunny twittered over in the approved manner . . . 'Oh, gorgeous! Oh, isn't he sweet! And so like you!'

Sue put the photograph back, beaming with maternal pride.

'I'm sorry it smells a bit like a French brothel in here,' said the Jungle Bunny.

'Well, it does rather, doesn't it?'

'I'm afraid Henry upset my perfume.'

'Did he?' They both turned to smile at Henry. 'He is a little clumsy sometimes,' Sue said, apologetically.

By this time, and all things considered, there was not a great deal of Henry's masculine dignity extant but what there was came rapidly to the conclusion that it could take no more. Being sophisticated about marital infidelity was all very well but this was fast becoming ludicrous. He therefore let out an anguished howl of protest.

'What the hell's going on here?' he yelled. ' "Have a cigarette" – "No, have one of mine" – "Look at this picture of my baby" – "Ooh, isn't he lovely?" What *is* this – a bloody tea party? Why aren't you tearing each other's hair out? Why aren't you . . . why aren't you *fighting*?'

Sue and the Jungle Bunny smiled comfortably at each other.

'Actually, I'd thought of that,' Sue said. 'But I didn't know whether it would do any good. Well, you see, I've not had any experience of this sort of thing and I wasn't sure how to go about it, really.'

'You're handling it very well,' the Jungle Bunny said graciously.

'Am I? Oh, thank you. I expect . . . well, I mean, I suppose you've known this kind of situation before, have you?'

The Jungle Bunny shook her head. 'No.'

'Really? Well, you're doing awfully well, too, if I may say so.'

'Well, it's best to be civilized about these things, don't you think?'

'Oh, I do.' Sue perched herself elegantly on the edge of the armchair and the Jungle Bunny leaned against the chest of drawers with her legs crossed at the ankle and one hip outthrust in an unconsciously erotic pose. In their contrasting ways they were both extremely attractive women.

Henry, however, was in no mood to appreciate the fact. 'Civilized!' he said bitterly. 'This is positively decadent. You're talking about me as if I was a bloody lap-dog or something.'

Sue turned to him soothingly. 'It's no good getting excited darling. The only sensible way is to sort the whole thing out as amicably as possible.'

'Oh, is it? Well, what if the situation was reversed and I was discussing you with some other bloke? Would you expect us to be amicable?'

'No, I should expect you to hit him.'

'Then why don't you hit her?' he cried.

'Because this is different. Isn't it?' she asked the Jungle Bunny.

'Of course, it is,' said the Jungle Bunny. 'Would you like some coffee?'

'Not at the moment, thank you.'

'I'd like some,' said Henry sulkily.

They ignored him. 'To tell you the truth,' said Sue, 'I was a bit worried about charging in here. It could have been awfully embarrassing, especially if . . .' She nodded towards the bed. 'Well, you know.'

'That would have been awful,' said the Jungle Bunny, shuddering.

'One would have looked such a fool. Well, you know that joke where the man finds his wife in bed with someone else and says "Keep still while I'm talking to you"? It could have been just like that.'

All at once she began to giggle and so did the Jungle Bunny. Henry went all hot and said: 'Oh, my God!'

'It's a funny thing,' Sue went on, 'but I was madly jealous before I met you and now I'm not. Oh, dear, I hope that doesn't sound insulting.'

'No-o-o,' said the Jungle Bunny, thoughtfully. 'I think I know what you mean.'

'It's just that I should have hated him to fall into the clutches of some awful little tart.'

The Jungle Bunny gave this an earnest nod of approval. 'Oh no, he's much too nice for that.'

'Oh, Jesus!' said Henry. He could take no more. He buttoned his jacket, picked up his raincoat and started to walk out.

'Where are you going?' Sue asked.

'I don't know,' he said, with deep bitterness. 'Just as far as I can possibly get from the pair of you. I've had you both up to here. It's *me* you're talking about, you know. How do you think I feel, hearing you treacling away like a pair of cackling Solomons, splitting me down the middle?'

'We're just trying to be *sensible*,' said Sue.

'Well, go on being sensible then but don't expect me to stay here and listen. I'm shoving off and I'm going to make up my own mind whether I want to see either of you again and in the meantime you can both go to hell.'

Before they could reply he was out of the room and slamming the door behind him.

Thirty seconds later he came back. 'I say,' he said. 'Can anyone lend me a couple of quid? I've only got sixty-seven pence on me.'

The two women exchanged tolerant little smiles. 'Come along, darling,' Sue said. 'Let's go home.'

'No, I'm damned if I . . .'

'Why not? We can talk it over together quietly and you can still walk out again if you want to.'

'Well . . .' Henry said doubtfully.

'Yes, do,' said the Jungle Bunny. 'You go home with Sue. It's much the most sensible thing.'

Henry stared at her with hatred. He stared at them both with hatred and for a moment he contemplated the idea of putting the pair of them across his knee and smacking their backsides soundly. It was an attractive notion and he knew that, in one way, it was precisely what he ought to do. But, in another way, he knew it would do no good and he doubted in any case whether they would understand what had made him do it.

Because he was the guilty one. There was no question about that. He had not treated either of them very well and with this knowledge ever close to the surface of his mind he found it impossible to allow himself the luxury of indignation and wrath, even in the face of the humiliation he had suffered.

Not, in any case, that they had intended to humiliate him. He was sure of that. No doubt they both felt, in their eccentric female fashion, that they had behaved splendidly in what could have been a nasty situation and had succeeded in putting right, without tears or bloodshed, what he, the lumbering male oaf, had put wrong. The fact that he found their patience and reasonableness screamingly intolerable was probably just further evidence of his own unworthiness.

Humiliation and anger faded and guilt and shame took their place. And instead of bringing the palm of his hand smartly to bear on the Jungle Bunny's nearly naked bottom and then doing the same thing to his wife, he took a deep breath and mumbled: 'All right, then. Let's go home.'

27. A SMALL FAVOUR

Mark Payne was still waiting in his car. A Lamborghini, naturally. His spectacles glinted with deep sincerity in the light of a street-lamp as Henry went by, but he didn't speak.

When they had gone twenty yards further on, Henry turned to look back. Mark was walking up the steps to the Jungle Bunny's house.

'Who's that?' Sue asked.

'Mark Payne.'

'Really? Oh!' She thought about it for a second or two. 'He was waiting for you to leave so that he . . . ?'

'That's right.'

'Poor old boy,' she said, laying a hand tenderly on his arm. 'You have had a rotten time, haven't you?'

'Pretty rotten,' he said.

Sue had parked their car round the corner and when they reached it he noted, without rancour – almost with resignation as if this were the natural order of things – that she moved automatically into the driving seat. He took his place beside her without a murmur of protest.

Maybe, he thought, that was the way it ought to be – she in the driver's seat and he as the passenger. And even if this was not the way it ought to be, those were the roles they had adopted and it was going to be hard to change them now.

He studied her covertly as she drove with swift efficiency towards the West End. Her expression was calm, contented and just a little bit triumphant, the expression of a victor, and he was under no illusions about the fact that the victory had not been over the Jungle Bunny but over him.

The car sped swiftly through the almost deserted streets of early morning London, the only capital in the world that goes to bed at eleven p.m. and thinks it sinful to be about after midnight.

'You all right?' he asked.

'Yes, fine thanks.'

Yes, of course she was. Because she had won, she had taken over. He wondered, broodingly, what had happened to all that big talk of his about male emancipation. That had died at a very young age. Big joke, really. Big, sad joke. When it came to a direct confrontation with women it was as much as the average man could do to survive, never mind about exert his authority. Henry had survived, though only just, but his woolly efforts in the direction of self-emancipation had led only to deeper enslavement.

'What have you done about Timmy?' he asked.

'Left him with Lorna Collins. She thinks I had to come and meet you at a night club.'

'Oh.' He fell silent. Then . . . 'How did you know where to find me?'

'Morgan told me.'

'That bastard.'

Am I really jealous of Sue? Henry wondered, remembering. Yes, probably. Am I an underdog? Again yes, probably. But can I change, that's the thing? Is it too late?

He was thirty-five years old and where had he got to? Nowhere really. His wife was more successful than he was, more capable, too. Sue would never have got into the kind of mess he'd been in all week. And if she had, he would never have been able to extricate her as successfully as she had extricated him. And extricated he was. For it was all over now. He was back and she had fetched him back, rather like a mother retrieving a runaway child, perhaps, but with love and a genuine desire to have him back, for all that.

'She's a nice girl, isn't she?' Sue said.

'Eh? Who?'

'Maria. You know. Who did you think I meant?'

Maria. Was that her name? Another twinge of guilt. They had never properly been introduced and he had never thought to ask her what she was called. Maria. Nice name. It suited her.

'Yes.' he said. 'Yes, she is.'

'I liked her.'

'So I gathered.'

They were driving through the suburbs now, past dark and sleeping houses in which respectable married couples snored peacefully side by side.

'You didn't mind my butting in like that, did you?' she asked.

'No. Just as well, really.'

'Because . . . well, I do love you. Very much. And I couldn't let you go just like that, not without trying to keep you. It was daft of me to walk out on you, only I thought it was what you wanted, you see.'

'Yes.'

'I do love you,' she said again.

'I love you, too.'

So he did, and perhaps that was the trouble. She was bright and intelligent and very pretty and feminine and much too efficient for him. What he really needed was someone less capable and more clinging but he hadn't got anyone like that. He'd got Sue and he loved her and she loved him and he was thirty-five years old and he hadn't got anywhere and if he didn't start doing something pretty damn soon he'd never get anywhere. A cloud of instant gloom settled upon him. Perhaps, it would have been best if he'd ended it all . . .

'You weren't thinking of committing suicide again in the morning, were you?' Sue asked telepathically.

'What?'

'Only I've thrown your razor away. I got you an electric one as a present.'

'Thank you.' Oh, well. Maybe, after all, fighting back was better. It only needed a little guts. He could have another go at that novel of his. He could make a fresh demand, now that Coughlin was gone, for a transfer to the features staff. He could start asserting himself a little more at home. He could . . .

Sue pulled into the driveway of their little house and cut the engine. 'Home,' she said, brightly.

'Yeah.' The rain had stopped and it was a pleasant night, cool and starry. Henry started to get out of the car.

'Darling,' she said. 'I was wondering . . . I'm going to be rather busy in the morning and . . . I was wondering if you'd do the school run for me.'

He settled back in his seat and stared out of the window for a long moment. Well, why not? She'd taken him back forgiven him for being a bloody fool, hadn't uttered a word of recrimination all the way home. She'd been marvellous, really marvellous. He must have hurt her very badly and yet she was behaving, well, like a saint. And after all, what was she asking of him? A small enough favour, for heaven's sake. He wouldn't even have to get up specially early to do it. He had enough time before he went to work to do two school runs. Of course, it would become a regular thing, he had no doubt of that. As soon as he had done it once, Sue would make sure that he did it again and again. He could just imagine the school run rota that the women drew up and circulated among themselves, with the dates and the list of names – Diana, Betty, Valerie, Christine, Samantha, Henry, Emma . . . Well, he owed it to her, didn't he? It would be another defeat in a long series of defeats but . . .

He sighed, swallowed heavily and turned towards her.

'No, I bloody well won't,' he said.

There was a pause and then she chuckled in the darkness beside him. 'I was hoping you'd say that,' she said and twined her arms around his neck.